EDUCE

BLACK CLOVERS MC #2

A. GORMAN

Educe

Copyright © 2022 A. Gorman.

ALL RIGHTS RESERVED.

This work of fiction is protected under International and Federal Copyright Laws and Treaties. Any unauthorized reprint or use of this material is prohibited. No part of this book may be reproduced or transmitted in any form or by any means, electronic or mechanical, including photocopying, recording, or by any information storage and retrieval system without express written permission from the author, A. Gorman, except where permitted by law.

The author acknowledges the trademarks status and trademark owners of various products referenced in this work of fiction have been used without permission. The use of these trademarks is not authorized, associated with, or sponsored by the trademark owners.

PUBLISHED IN THE UNITED STATES OF AMERICA

Cover design by Charlie Fields
Edited by Kim Lubbers
Proofread by Leah Pugh
Formatting/Interior text design by Jennifer Laslie

The characters and events portrayed in this book are fictitious. Names, characters, places, and incidents are the product of the author's imagination. Any resemblance to actual persons, living or dead, business establishments, events, or locales is entirely coincidental.

BLACK CLOVERS MC

Prez: Brandon "Sledge" Lewis
Ol' lady – Dr. Ava Swartz
VP: John "VPeep" Peeples
Ol' lady – Scarlett Peeples
Sergeant At Arms: Mike "Tyson" Woodford
Ol' lady – Lana Ray
Treasure: James "Cash" Sharp
Ol' lady – June Sharp
Children – Johnny, Keith, Waylon
Secretary/ Sharpshooter: Seth "Snaps" Napleton
Enforcer: Ronan "Warrior" Hubbard
Children – Mason and Madison
Tech: Ian "Robo" Robertson
Medic: Willis "Striker" Kuhn
Chaplin: Thomas "Preach" Ross
Prospect: Wolf
Prospect: Lucky
Prospect: Raider
Prospect: Wardog
Prospect: Bandit
Prospect: Pappy

PROLOGUE

Three months ago

Warrior

"I pronounce you husband and wife. You may kiss your bride," the pastor states, and the church gets loud.

I smile as I cup my hands on Kelsey's face, kissing her deeply. Hoots and hollers echo around us, and I feel like I'm the luckiest man in the world. This wedding has been years in the making, and we finally got here today.

"I present to you Mr. and Mrs. Ronan Hubbard," the pastor states, and applause thunders around us.

We walk down the flower-petal-filled aisle, and my friends and family slap me on the back. They know this is the happiest day of my life. Kelsey and I go to the assigned area away from where the doors of the sanctuary so we can greet everyone who attended our wedding as they leave. I kiss her again, not holding back.

"I can't wait to get you all to myself tonight," I whisper in her ear.

"Why is that?" She grins, knowing she's dying for me to be beside her.

"So, I can show you how hard you got me… You in that dress, I'd fuck you now if we didn't have four hundred people getting ready to see us." I groan.

"I can't wait to rub up on you during our dance." She smirks.

"You wouldn't?"

"But I would. I'd enjoy watching you squirm in front of our families with your raging hard on."

"I'll fuck you in the bathroom of the reception hall."

"You wouldn't!" She gasps.

"I will. I've waited too long to be inside of you, Mrs. Hubbard. As soon as we get to the hall, I'm ripping those panties off and fucking you in this dress."

"Well, I'm not wearing any panties, so you have easy access." She winks.

"Oh, baby. That's a nice little surprise."

"Yes, now behave. The people are coming, and we don't want them to spoil our plans." She kisses my lips quickly as our parents are at the front of the line. They gave us best wishes, hugs, and kisses, then told us they would meet at the reception hall.

The line goes on forever, but we get to the reception, where we quickly find the restroom. I lock the door, push her against the door, and kiss her roughly.

"All I've been thinking about is being buried in your pussy. Making you scream my name as I make you come."

"I've missed you being inside of me… fuck me already, and tonight we will take it slow."

"Already bossy, I see." I unzip my pants and push them down to free my cock and balls, and take my dick in my palm, making sure it's hard. "Lift your dress."

Kelsey smirks, but she does as I ask, revealing her freshly waxed bush in the shape of a heart.

"Cute." I grin as I pick her up. "Wrap your legs around me, baby." She wraps her legs around my waist, and I slide her down onto my hardened cock and thrust into her. I close my eyes as I pound into my wife, her orgasm building, tightening her hold on my cock with each thrust.

Her moans fill the room as bullets zoom past our heads. With Kelsey in my arms, I drop as the shots ring out. The room shakes, bricks and dust fly around us. What the fuck is happening? I look down at Kelsey, and she's dead. Blood soaks through her wedding dress.

I scream for help as I lose my shit, and I look

around. I'm no longer at the wedding reception. The lights flicker. Darkness surrounds me. I'm no longer holding Kelsey. My Army-issued rifle has replaced her.

"Move out," the voice yells out from behind me.

I move. But I can't see where I'm moving to, so I run. I'm running and running until I come to the bright light. Finally, I'll be able to see. The white light is getting brighter and brighter, but I'm finally there. There's someone in the white light, and when I see them, my knees give out, and I hit the ground.

"You couldn't save me. No one could," Kelsey says as she holds a rusted razor blade to her arm, then slices upward. I try to stop the bleeding, but there's so much blood. I cry out for help, and I get up and run, trying to find help, and as I open the door, I walk through, but there isn't a floor there, and I fall and fall—

"Fuck!" I gasp as I jolt out of bed and rub my face with my hands. The nightmares have consumed my sleep for the last couple of nights. They always get bad near the anniversary of her death, especially knowing I could have saved her if I were here…

I roll out of bed, knowing I won't be able to go back to sleep and check on the kids. It will be eight years since they've seen their mother; only Madison remembers her. Mason was a baby when she died.

Her death was the first of several the club faced in a short period, forever changing us.

I shower and head downstairs for coffee. I make it to the kitchen, and Snaps is pouring himself a cup.

"Want one?" He holds up the pot.

"Please."

"You look like shit, man," he says as he places a cup of coffee down in front of me.

"I couldn't sleep."

"Nightmares back?" he asks as he sits across from me.

"Yeah. The anniversary is coming up."

"I couldn't imagine… but maybe it's time you moved on. Put your dick inside of someone else."

"Whenever I try to move on with someone else, I can't. I can't even fuck a clubwhore."

"Almost eight years of jacking off. How does your hand still work?" He smirks. "Maybe you'll meet the right girl, and everything will change for you."

"I doubt it. Kind of hard to find a woman when you're not looking for one, and you're busy raising two kids in an MC."

"You never know, man." He takes a sip of his coffee. "After Tyson gets in, we have church."

"Okay," I say before downing the coffee, the warmth waking me up. "I need to get the kids ready for school. I'll talk to you later."

I take the stairs two at a time, hoping the kids wake up in good moods because it will make the day easier. Madison is the hardest to wake up, so I go into her room first and gently attempt to wake her up.

"Stop, Dad," she grumbles.

"Madison, you need to get up for school."

"No, I'm dead inside. I don't want to." She throws the covers over her head.

"Madison, you have fifteen minutes to get up and ready, or I'll send June in here." June and Cash have three boys; she can get them rounded up in seconds. She's scary.

"Nooo, Dad."

"Then get up."

"Okay, I will." She throws the covers off her and scowls at me.

"I'll be back to check on you in fifteen minutes." I chuckle.

She yawns. "I'll be ready."

I walk out of the room and head to Mason's room. I knock on the door and go in, flipping on the light, and he's not in bed. What the hell? I look around, and the door to the bathroom opens.

"Hey, Dad," he says as he gets back into bed, dressed.

"Why are all the lights out?"

"You're always on us for leaving every light on, so I turn off the lights when showering."

"Oh. It's time to get up and dressed for school."

"I'm ready. I have to get my shoes on," Mason says as he stretches under the covers and throws them off.

"Okay, get them on, and we will go downstairs and get breakfast."

"Can we have pancakes and bacon?"

"You got it because it sounds good." I leave his room and check on Madison.

I knock on her door.

"I'm coming!" she shouts.

"You have five minutes, Mads." I sigh as I see Mason walking down the hallway with everything he'll need for school, but only if they were both that easy.

CHAPTER
ONE

The Day Before...

Rosalina

"Natalia, I don't understand why you need me to go to Texas. It's pretty clear that Tyson wanted nothing to do with you. His girlfriend's pretty nice, but you wouldn't know that because you were too busy trying to hook up with her boyfriend."

"These guys don't keep women long. I'm sure that since they're back home, they are no longer an item." Natalia grins.

"I think you're wrong," I state, knowing their relationship was solid before they went home.

"I've made a few friends that will ensure she's no longer in my way." She snickers.

"Putada! What have you done?" Worry consumes

me because I know how vindictive Natalia can be to get what she wants.

"Nothing... too bad. Have your things ready by tonight. We'll head to Texas first thing in the morning."

"Okay, if you say so. Did you get it cleared with my brother?" I question her, knowing she's heading for an all-time low.

"I'll talk to him in a bit," she says as she gets up from the couch and leaves my apartment. I don't trust her to talk to my brother, so I get my phone from the charger and call him.

"Hey, what's up?" Ramiro answers.

"Not much. Natalia wants me to go to Texas with her." I sigh.

"Do you know what for?"

"She has it in her head that she can break up Tyson and Lana." I hate feeling like a tattletale, but whatever she's doing could cause trouble for the MC. I won't be a part of that. "She said something about making friends that would help her eliminate Lana."

He says nothing.

"Ramiro?"

"I'm here." The line goes silent again with a click. He's muting his phone because he doesn't want me to hear what he is saying to whoever is in the room with him. The line clicks again. "Go with her to Texas. Let me know if she meets anyone outside of the club. Don't be afraid to go to Sledge, either. He will make sure you are safe," he breathes out.

"Okay? Are you sure? Because it isn't like you to let me go off without you."

"I trust you'll do the right thing, Rosalina. Stay out of trouble."

"You know I will."

"Te quiero, hermana."

"Te quiero," I reply instantly and end the call.

I didn't expect the call to go like that, and I fall back onto the couch. My brother doesn't like me to be too far from home, which makes me believe there are ulterior motives behind our going to Texas. My brother's very calculated with all he does. Ramiro didn't become the Vice President of the Black Clovers Mexico by being sloppy. No, he isn't like our father.

My father, Eliso Rodrígues, was a drug runner for the cartel and came to America, where he met my mother. They fell in love and got married. My brother and I were born and raised in Arizona. My father was on the run from federal agents and went back to Mexico to hide when I was in Middle School.

While in high school, Ramiro spent four years in the Marines and got out when I graduated. He wanted to go to Mexico and spend time with our father and his family, and I tagged along because I didn't know what I wanted to do after high school. College wasn't appealing to me, but I knew I needed to do something.

We arrived in Mexico, and I never looked back. I miss my mom and visit her when I can, but I didn't realize Mexico was the missing piece of me. The moment I stepped onto the soil here, I felt at home. My mom, Susann, didn't like that I stayed here, but she understood. I asked her to move to Mexico with her family... and she said she needed to stay in the States and maintain her business; she owns a personal finance company.

My father has an upholstery business, but it's a front for his illegal businesses. I don't know what all he is into, and I don't want to either. I know Ramiro keeps me protected, but I don't know all I need to be protected from, which brings me back to why he is letting me go to Texas. I understand that the club there will keep me safe, but there are many unknowns.

I get up from the couch and go to my room to pack for an extended trip because who knows how long I will have to babysit her in Texas.

The drive to Texas isn't bad. We pull up, and a club party is in full swing. Of course, Natalia would want to come while they were having a party. Pappy shows us where we are staying while we're here. It's different from the club at home because they put us in a guest suite. We aren't staying with the putas, which is where our guests stay at home.

"This place is so much nicer. I can't wait to make it my home," Natalia gushes.

"What makes you think this will work out in your favor?" I raise an eyebrow and bite my lip, wanting to say more.

"If I can't get him now, I'll get him later." She claps her hands. "Lana has a hit out on her, and I'm making sure it's carried out." She giggles with excitement.

"Natalia Alvarez! Why would you do that?" Horror fills my body, and my hands shake. She's a monster.

"Because when I see something I want, I make sure I get it, no matter the cost." She smirks.

"I don't know how I could be friends with someone so evil," I spit out.

"I'm not evil. I'm aggressive. I don't sit around and wait for things to happen—I make things happen. When the opportunity presented itself, I took advantage of it." She shrugs.

"It's not right." I shake my head, knowing that shit is going to hit the fan when they find out what she's been up to behind closed doors.

"By whose standards? Because all is fair game in the MC life."

"If all this happens, how are you going to live with yourself, knowing that you helped kill someone?"

"I'll sleep very well wrapped in Tyson's arms in his bed." Natalia laughs.

I don't know what to say to her; how do you respond to something like that? I have a feeling that

Ramiro knows about Natalia and her betrayal, but I need to make sure he knows all this.

"Are you ready? I want to get there before the party is over," she whines.

"Yes, I'm as ready as I'll ever be." I feel like I'm going to throw up.

We leave the room, and Pappy stands outside the door, waiting for us. I don't know how much he heard, and I give him a nervous smile. He smiles back.

"This way to the clubhouse, ladies," he states as he points toward the larger building in the middle of the compound.

"Thank you," Natalia states, then smiles.

Pappy opens the door, and we walk into silence. A catcall rings out, and I look around. They are staring at us, and I see Tyson and Lana. Her eyes narrow as she sees Natalia walk through the clubhouse. I watch Tyson leave Lana's side and walk over to talk to several other guys. One of them looks up at me, and chills run through my body.

He's the most gorgeous man I've ever seen. I usually felt nothing for MC guys, but he does something to me. Natalia grabs my arm, pulling my focus from Tyson and the others in the opposite direction.

We walk up to the bar and get a drink.

"Once that putada leaves, then I'm going over to Tyson and remind him what he is missing out on," she smugly states.

"If you say, Natalia." I roll my eyes.

I feel like someone is watching me, and I take a sip of my drink and look around the room, my eyes meeting the gorgeous man I saw earlier. He smirks, and I lose all train of thought.

"I'll be back, Natalia," I say as I approach him.

"Hey,"

"Hey, yourself. So, your Jaguar's little sister?"

"Yes. I'm Rosalina."

"Nice to meet you. I'm Warrior. What are you doing with Natalia? She's drama."

"I'm asking myself that very question." I roll my eyes and look back at where I'd left Natalia. She's no longer standing there. I scan the room and see Natalia sitting on Tyson's lap.

"That isn't good." I point over at Natalia and Tyson.

"Oh, fuck. Lana is going to beat her ass." He laughs.

I watch Natalia, and she's leaning over, trying to place her cleavage in Tyson's face, but he isn't having anything to do with her. Something catches my eye, and I see Lana coming toward them. Her face is red with anger. Lana grabs Natalia's ponytail and yanks her onto the floor.

"I don't know how many times you have to be told, but Tyson is off-limits. He's mine. I laid claim to him long before your skank ass came into the picture."

Natalia stands up, lunging at her. Lana moves to the left and swings her right hand, connecting with her nose. She stumbles back, and Lana swings her left fist and connects with her jaw.

"If you're going to fuck with a Princess, you better make sure you know which one you're fucking with. I grew up on the streets of Chicago. I won't roll over because someone else wants my man. I fight for what's mine. So, if you want me to keep kicking your ass, then stand up and fight like a woman. If not, stay down like the dog you are," she grits out, waiting for her to make a move. Natalia crawls away from her. "Crawl back to Mexico, bitch."

I stand frozen in place, and Warrior wraps his arm around my shoulders.

"Tyson, take your girl upstairs to calm down," Sledge sternly states. "Striker, take care of Natalia. Rosalina, I need to talk to you in my office *now*."

Fuck, fuck, fuck.

"This way," Warrior says as he doesn't remove his arm and guides me to the office.

We are the only two in there for a moment, and then two others come in.

"Welcome to Texas, Rosalina. I'm Sledge, the President of this chapter. I see you've met Warrior, and this is Robo. Jaguar said you would let us know if Natalia said or did anything out of the normal... I'm not asking you to rat out your friend. I'm asking you to give me any information I might need to keep my family safe."

I sit there, not sure what to say. The guilt of betraying Natalia weighs heavily on me, but I need to say something if I can stop Lana from getting hurt. So, I take a deep breath, hoping to calm my nerves.

"She's been working with someone to make sure they take Lana out of the picture… they are going to kill her. Lana has a hit out on her," I rush out.

"Thank you, Rosalina. I know it's hard, but you are saving a life. I'll let Jaguar know, too."

"Okay." I nod, not knowing what else to say.

I close my eyes and pray I can talk Natalia into going home to avoid this all.

CHAPTER **TWO**

Warrior

I watch Rosalina struggle as she talks to Sledge about the bitch that's trying to kill a member of our MC and an ol' lady. That shit doesn't fly with the Black Clovers, and with her being Alvarez's niece, she doesn't get special treatment. A traitor is a traitor, and she'll be taken out. Everything will have to be planned, making sure that no one else is harmed in the crossfire.

She closes her eyes, and I know she's trying to compose herself. She takes a deep breath and lets it out as she opens her eyes. "Can I check on Natalia now?"

"Yes, Pappy will take you to the clinic," Sledge states, pulling me, watching every move she makes. "Rosalina."

"Yes?" She looks up at Sledge.

"Don't mention this conversation to Natalia." His tone is commanding.

"I won't, sir."

"Thank you." He nods, dismissing her.

She gives me a small smile and stands, leaving the office.

"Do you think she left anything out?" Sledge asks, looking at me.

"No, I think Jaguar instilled in her that family comes before friendships."

"Monitor her, though. Whomever Natalia is working with might come after her."

"Will do."

"Robo, can you access Natalia's call records, emails, and whereabouts?"

"On it, I'll let you know what I find," Robo states as he puts information into his phone. "I'll have something in the morning for you."

"I'll let you get to it," Sledge says, dismissing him.

"We didn't need this shit on top of Harms Deliver." He sighs and puts his feet on the desk.

"I know..."

"I've known Natalia since she was a little girl, Warrior. This fucking sucks. My dad and Alvarez were tight." Sledge closes his eyes. I know he's thinking of his dad and how his dad would handle this situation.

I give him a moment.

"Alvarez is the one that told us she was giving up club secrets to a rival MC... He's loyal to his Black

Clovers family over his blood family." His eyes open, and he looks at me.

"Yes, he is because he was a founding member along with my dad, uncles, and Brady." Sledge has aged a lot over the past few years. Living the lifestyle we do does that to a person. "We need to find out when they are planning on taking the hit out on Lana and let Slasher and Tyson know so we can develop a solid plan."

"After what happened with Lana and Natalia, she will contact whomever and set up the plans so she isn't in the crossfire."

"We'll see what Robo returns with and go from there."

"All right. Let me know what you need from me when we get intel. I'll start working on a plan tonight and will review it with Tyson tomorrow. We need to cover all our bases."

"Yea, we do. See you in the morning," he states as he places his boots on the floor and stands.

We leave his office, and I pull my phone from my pocket. The kids are spending the night at friends' houses, which I'm glad. Enough is going on here without Natalia's drama. I'll have to keep them away from here until it's decided how we'll deal with her.

I text them both, *'Good night, I love you,'* and they instantly respond with *'I love you'* before I can make it to my room.

Thoughts of Kelsey flood my mind, hoping she is proud of how I've raised our kids, but Rosalina replaces them as I undress and lie down in bed. She's gorgeous, and when I placed my arm around her shoulders, warmth radiated throughout my body, going straight to my dick.

Maybe Snaps is right. Fucking someone could be what I need, but I'm not dumb enough to fuck a brother's sister and be done with her. None of the whores that live at the club do anything for me, either. After years of trying, they stay away, which is fine by me. I've talked to Chloe, Sofia, and Phoebe a little, but they stick to themselves, along with Savannah.

There's something going on between Snaps and her, but they keep it quiet, whatever it is, because Sledge will cut off Snaps' dick if he hurts Savannah. I chuckle to myself because the club is like a damn soap opera some days.

Rosalina is a breath of fresh air, which is exactly what the club needs right now. What I need, I think, as I close my eyes and think of Rosalina under me, moaning out my name.

I spend Saturdays with the kids, but since they are away, I'll meet with Tyson, since Robo could get a lot of information about who Natalia was supplying with intel. She's made a lot of calls and texts to St. Louis over the past few months. Robo could see messages from last night after the fight, and she was telling Brandon that Lana was so mean to her, and she was beaten up for coming here… blah, blah, blah. The bitch lied in all the messages Robo could download, and I believe she doesn't know where the truth ends and the lies began. Delusional bitch.

Tyson's going to flip his shit when he reads everything. He knows she's a skank, but I don't think we realized how deep Natalia has dug herself in with the Ivory Wolves. I read through everything again, and I throw the file on the table and stand up. Looking at my watch, Tyson should be here in ten minutes, giving me enough time to grab coffee.

I go to the kitchen and return to the conference room, where Tyson is already reading the file. His ears are blood red, and his hands are trembling. I don't know if it's from anger, their sustained damage, or both. I sit across the table from him and wait for him to speak.

He slams his fists down, rubbing his hand before he speaks. "You know how hard it'll be to keep someone on Lana twenty-four-seven? I'm gonna kill Natalia with my bare hands," he seethes.

"We have to use her like she's using us, bro."

"Do you have any thoughts on how to lure them into a trap?" He looks up at me, anger threatening to take over his body.

"I have a few ideas, but they could be risky."

"If we don't create some type of diversion, Lana could end up dead, and I don't want to go down that road again because I don't know if I'll survive without her."

"You're fully committed to her? I know you claimed her as your ol' lady, but?"

"Yeah. I'm doing it right, too. She's going to be my wife. I just have to get the balls up to ask her. I will eventually." His expression softens. He's in love. I remember the look all too well, and it's a kick in the gut, but I don't like my emotions showing.

"I'm happy for ya, bro." I smile, glad that he's found someone to make him happy.

"Just another reason I'd do anything to keep her safe," he says with anger still present in his words.

"One of my thoughts was to plan a party and let Natalia 'help plan it' so she knows all the details, but she won't know everything," as I say it, I don't know how well this workout—too many unknowns.

"You could be onto something there." He takes his hand and rubs his mouth, thinking about my thoughts.

"Yea. Lana and Scarlett graduate from college in three months. We could have an enormous party at Kilkenny's… and let Slasher and his bunch know about our plans so they can come in and help us handle business."

"I'm like the sound of this, and we can ambush them if everything falls into place."

"Definitely. Let's work out this idea fully and then

devise two other operation plans we can give to Sledge. We can't let any ladies know about our plans because one slip and Natalia would know that we are on to her."

"I might need to include Rosalina. I don't want her to be in the line of fire trying to protect her friend."

"That's going to have to be a Sledge call." He pauses as he looks at me. "The look on your face tells me you're in your head about her… but Jaguar is very protective of his little sister. I would proceed with caution if I were you." He smirks.

"I can look. She's hot… and everything." Shit. I didn't think I was that transparent.

"And she's single." He sits back, relaxing back into the chair.

"How do you know?" I smirk, shaking my head.

"She and Lana spent some time together, and from what I gathered, Jaguar ran off anyone who came around sniffing."

"Interesting."

He laughs.

"What?"

"I can't believe it's taken a twenty-four-year-old to pull you out of your eight-year dry spell…"

"I wouldn't go that far."

"Keep kidding yourself." He snickers.

"Let's get back to flushing out Natalia, and then I can think about what to do about Rosalina."

CHAPTER
THREE

Rosalina

After a month in Texas, I thought I would miss being home in Mexico, but I was wrong. While I've been here, I've met several ladies and tried to distance myself from Natalia, but it has been hard. Savannah, Sledge's sister, pulled me into her ring of friends. They were rescued with Tyson, and they stayed here because the club makes sure they're safe from the MC that kidnapped them. Lana and I talk, too, but Dr. Swartz keeps her busy at the clinic.

In the four years my brother has been involved with the club, I've learned the Black Clovers protect their own, but if you betray their trust, there is no gaining it back. I'm worried about what's going to happen to Natalia... but she gets what she deserves. She grew up in the club as the niece of one of the founding members but has disrespected the very foundation of the club. Family first. Instead, she put herself before the safety of the club. Ramiro told me she won't be coming back to Mexico alive.

I knew the club would take care of her, but I didn't know when or where, so I've been trying to stay away from her. I don't need to be punished for her sins, too, because I had to betray her, and guilt washes over me. Am I any better than Natalia?

"You keep thinking that hard, your brain might explode."

I open my eyes and look up. Warrior is pouring himself a cup of coffee and looks over to me.

"Need a refill?"

I look down at my empty cup and nod. He leans over and refills my cup, and I watch his muscles work under his tight shirt, and his cologne invades my space. I close my eyes and think about how his body would feel on mine.

"You okay?" he asks as he sits across the table, pulling me from my daydream.

"Yes, just thinking about home," I lie.

"Miss it?"

"Not as much as I thought I would. Ramiro hovers over me like he's my mother, so here I have a little more freedom to do what I want to do."

"Nice." He takes a sip of his coffee. "Madison said you helped with her homework last night."

"Yes, I loved biology in school. She's a really sweet girl."

"Thanks. I wonder some days because she's always telling me she's dead inside."

I giggle. "Most girls are that age. At least she talks to you. I don't think I talked to my mom much during my seventh-grade year."

"She growls at me most of the time."

"Oh my. I'm sure it will get better."

"I hope so." He clears his throat. "Have a good day. I need to get some things done."

"Okay. Talk to you later."

"Bye." He smiles as he gets up and walks out of the kitchen, and my eyes focus on his ass.

I'm not this person. One whom a man turns on, but there's something about him that pulls me to him. But that's not why I'm here. I know that as soon as they decide how to deal with Natalia and it's completed, I'll be back on my way home.

A feeling I can't explain takes over my body, and I'm hesitant to return to Mexico for the first time since I left America.

"Ugh." I groan as I realize I have a crush on Warrior.

"Hey, Lina!" Savannah says as she enters the kitchen, snapping me from beating myself up internally. "Warrior said you were in here. Do you want to go shopping with us today?"

"Um, where do you go shopping? Because what I've seen of here, there isn't much in town."

"We're going to Houston. If you can find Natalia, she can come, too."

"Sounds fun. Do we have a vehicle big enough for all of us?" Do I even want Natalia to go? She's such a downer, especially since I know everything I do.

"Yeah. We're taking the club SUV, and Snaps is going with us since Brandon doesn't want me to go too far without a leash." She rolls her eyes.

"I completely understand. Ramiro is the same way. I still can't believe he let me come here."

"Oh, I'm sure that if you stepped out of line, they would extend his hand through one of the other guys. We can't get away with anything."

"Exactly. I was told to stay out of trouble before I left, as if I could do anything to get into trouble."

"Preaching to the choir!" She giggles. "I'm going to finish getting ready. See you in about thirty minutes?"

"That works. I'll find Natalia and see if she wants to go."

She nods, takes the cup of coffee she poured while talking, and leaves the kitchen. I follow her and walk through the clubhouse, looking around to see who's about and who isn't. The common area is void of people, and I continue my way outside to the building I'm staying in. After the first night, we moved into separate rooms, which I appreciated so much. Being nice to her is fucking with my head, but I have to do what it takes to keep people safe.

I get to Natalia's room and hear talking on the other

side of the door, but I can't hear anyone responding. She must be on the phone, and I press my ear to the door to make out what is being said.

". . . graduation party. . . bar... details... I'm planning..."

What is she planning? I pull my ear away from the door and knock. The talking ceases, and I can hear her moving. She mumbles something else and then opens the door.

"Hey, girl. I was getting ready to call you to see where you were."

"I was in the clubhouse getting coffee. Savannah invited us to go shopping with them in Houston. I didn't know if you wanted to go."

"Who's all going?"

"I'm not sure. Probably Chloe, Sofia, Phoebe, but I'm not sure because I didn't ask."

"Hmm. I think I'll stay here because they asked me to help plan Scarlett and Lana's graduation party. I'm so excited and want to make sure it's perfect for them since they have worked hard through everything the past year."

"Oh, so you like Lana now?"

"Yes, I realize how immature I have been acting. I thought this would be a good way to make it up to her."

"That's good of you, Natalia. Are you sure you don't want to go shopping?"

"Yes, I'm sure. I need to talk to Mercy and Stephanie

about what we could do at Kilkenny's and get everything in order."

"Okay, have fun. See you soon."

"You too." She hugs me, and I know that she's lying. She might fool the others, but she's not fooling me.

"See you at dinner?"

"Of course." She smiles, and I want to punch her in the face.

I leave her room and go to mine, grabbing my things to meet Savannah and the rest of the girls outside of the clubhouse. They are all waiting for me when I arrive. Warrior is there, too. Is he coming with us?

"Snaps didn't want to be surrounded by women, so Warrior is coming along with us." Savannah chuckles. "We're too much for him."

"Oh, this will be fun." I wink at Savannah. Today might be the day I get into trouble.

We get into the SUV, and I sit next to Savannah and Phoebe. Sofia and Chloe sit at the very back. Savannah explained to me one day that the three of them were inseparable. When the guys found them, they were in cages, and it really messed with their heads. Savannah said she still has nightmares, but she's been talking to someone who has been helping her with her PTSD. She wishes the trio, as she calls them, would take Sledge's offer of seeing a psychologist, but they aren't ready. I hope they get the help they need.

"We're grabbing something to eat, too. I hope you

don't mind, but we always get Mexican…" Savannah bites her lip.

"Mmm. That sounds good. I've been missing it."

"Good, I'm sure it's nothing like what you have at home."

"I didn't know what authentic Mexican food was until I moved to Mexico six years ago. My mom is white as white can be, and she cooked nothing except meat and potatoes. My dad was too busy to show me how to cook traditional food. So, I grew up on takeout. I believe that's why I love living in Mexico so much. The ol' ladies are always cooking food. They invent reasons to celebrate, too." I giggle. "I put on fifteen pounds when Ramiro joined the MC because they always fed me."

"That's awesome. Maybe when you go back, I can visit you down there. Sounds different from here."

"It's a lot different, but there are things here that are better than in Mexico…" I feel someone watching me, and I look up in the rearview mirror and meet Warrior's eyes. I give him a small smile and watch as something flashes in his eyes. I can't tell what it is, especially since I can't see his face.

"I want to see that for myself." She smiles. "Especially if there is a beach close by…"

"Oh, there is. Laguna De Carpintero Tampico is my favorite place to go. Shopping, beach, and water all in one place."

"I'm coming home with you!" She laughs, and I look up to see the guys shaking theirs.

"We definitely can have some fun." I wink, and we both start laughing.

A half-hour later, we pull up to a cantina, and we all get out. As we walk in, I notice the sign for dollar margaritas. I point it out to Savannah, and she grins. We are thinking the same thing. Snaps and Warrior will have their hands full with both of us drinking.

CHAPTER **FOUR**

Warrior

"Don't you think you've had enough to drink?" I ask Savannah and Rosalina two hours after we arrived at the restaurant.

"No way, Warrior," Savannah slurs. "Lina needs another." The girls giggle, and Rosalina snorts. It's cute, but not cute enough to allow this shit to go on. I look at Snaps, and he's had enough.

"I'm going to send a video of this to Sledge," Snaps states as he stares Savannah down.

"You wouldn't?" Savannah gasps.

"Damn right, I would. So, we're going now."

"Fine. The shops aren't far from here, so drop us off there so we can be out of your hair."

"I don't think so, Savannah." He grits out. "I'm not letting you out of my sight."

I smirk because I know that she's trying him. He wants her so badly, and the feeling is mutual.

She huffs but says nothing, and Rosalina slinks into the booth because she knows if this gets back to Sledge, it'll get back to Jaguar, and she'll be in trouble. The others say little either because they have a good thing staying with us and don't want to do anything to jeopardize their new lives.

We finally leave the restaurant and drive to the shops. Shopping is the last thing I want to do, especially since Madison has been begging me to take her. I'm sure I won't hear the end of it when she finds out.

Shopping is uneventful as the girls sober up while walking through the shops. They say little to Snaps and me, but I catch Rosalina looking at me. She quickly looks away when our eyes meet. I don't know if she's afraid of me telling her brother what she did or if there's something else going on.

The girls see an ice cream shop and run to it, leaving Rosalina behind. I walk up beside her.

"Everything okay?"

"Um, yeah." She doesn't look at me, and I know she's lying.

"You're full of shit. Spill it."

She looks around, seeing that it's just her and I close by. "I overheard Natalia talking to someone but didn't catch all of it. I think it has to do with the graduation party she's planning."

"Hmm. Did she tell you she's planning the party?"

"Yes, then told me she reconsidered how she feels about Lana and has realized how immature she was acting." Rosalina stops walking and turns to me.

"Do you believe her?" I step closer to her, wanting to wrap her in my arms.

"No, not for a second. I think she's going to plan the party and tell whomever when and where everything is going to be to set Lana and the club up," she breathes out.

"I'm sure you're right, and that's what we are hoping for her to do." I wink.

"Oh, you're setting her up?"

"I'm not telling you because that way, it can't come back on you if you don't know." I look up to see the girls and Snaps standing in line at the ice cream shop.

"Thank you." Rosalina looks up, and our eyes meet.

"You're welcome. You have enough that you have to keep inside."

She wraps her arms around me, hugging me, and I freeze from the warmth of her body holding on to mine. I wrap my arms around her, holding her because I know she's feeling like her world is falling apart. Rosalina pulls away and takes a step back.

"I'm so sorry. I can't believe I did that." Her cheeks redden, and she looks down at her feet.

I close the distance between us, placing my back toward everyone where only she can see me, and take my fingers, tilting her chin up so she has to look me in the eyes. "Don't be sorry." I lean down and kiss her forehead.

She gasps, and I look down. Desire flashes in her eyes. My cock hardens as I think of the things I want to do to her. I close my eyes and take a breath in, inhaling her honeysuckle sweetness.

"Tell me I crossed the line," I mumble out, not thinking clearly.

She shakes her head, "No."

"This isn't the time or the place for this... but we're going to talk when we get back to the club."

"Okay," she breathes out softly.

"Hey, fucker! What kind of ice cream do you all want?" Snaps yells across the concourse. Idiot. Pulling Rosalina's body next to mine, I turn and walk to where they're waiting for us.

"Vanilla, you know that."

He pulls me off to the side. "I know I do. I didn't want you to do anything you would regret later."

"I'm good, bro." I wink and order my vanilla ice cream.

On the ride home, it doesn't take long for the girls to fall asleep, and it should be nice and quiet.

"What were you thinking back there, messing

around with Rosalina?" Snaps looks at me, then focuses back on the road.

"I could ask you the same thing about Savannah, but I already know the story."

"It's different." His head shakes.

"Hardly, fucker. You want to fuck Savannah, and I'm trying to figure out what I want to do with Rosalina." I smirk.

"You better keep your dick in your pants. Jaguar's protective of his little sister."

"Sounds familiar." I wink.

"Shut the fuck up," he snaps, then grins. "It's fucked up being in this situation."

"Yea. I spent most of my life stuck on Kelsey, and here I am, trying to figure this shit out. Like, what the fuck I'm feeling. I have no clue if she's feeling the same way because I've been out of the game too long."

"Bullshit, you fucking kissed her. It's obvious she's feeling some kind of way, too."

"We're going to talk when we get back to the clubhouse, if I think she's sober."

"She didn't drink that much. Savannah was slamming enough for both of them."

"I noticed. So, are you going to make your move on her?"

"When I think she's ready to have a relationship. She's still healing from being kidnapped, but she keeps telling me she's healed. I know better than that. You don't just magically heal PTSD, especially what they lived through."

"You might be waiting forever."

"That's okay. I've waited this long for her... I'll wait even longer." He gives me a half smile and focuses back on the road.

I lean my head back in the seat and close my eyes, thinking about Rosalina and the sound of her gasp going through me. My body hasn't reacted that way to anyone in a long time. I thought I was like Madison and dead inside, but Rosalina reminds me I'm a guy who likes to be with women... gorgeous women like her.

We arrive at the club, and the girls chat after their nap. Rosalina hangs back while the others go into the clubhouse.

"You feel like talking?" I ask her as I put a stray hair behind her ear.

"Yes, but can I take these bags to my room first?"

"I'll carry them for you." She hands them to me, and I take them, brushing her hand with my fingers.

"Thanks." She smiles.

We walk to her room in silence, and I wait for her outside of her room, because I don't know what I'd do if I see her and a bed in a same room. The things that went through my mind on the way back from Houston has my dick trying to do most of my thinking.

She meets me in the hallway. "Where do you want to talk?"

"Do you trust me?" I ask her as I take her hand in mine.

"Yes, why?"

"I'm going to take you to a place where we can talk with no one overhearing us."

"Okay."

We walk outside to my bike, and she looks at me. "We're going on your bike?"

"It's the best way to get there."

"Don't tell my brother. He won't allow me to ride on the back of another man's bike."

I laugh. "Yeah, it can mean some bad things in other MCs. Like for a ride, you have to give a blowjob or have sex."

Her eyes widen. "Are you serious?"

"Yeah. Didn't Jaguar tell you any of this?"

"No. He doesn't let me do anything unless it's with Diablo's wife, since she's ex-military. That's why I'm surprised I'm here."

"Well, no worries. We aren't that type of club, and I'm not that type of guy…"

She takes a step back.

"I'm kidding. Listen, I'm rusty at this. Please go for a ride with me? It's nothing more than that, I promise."

"Yes, thank you for asking." She smirks. Oh, she has a feisty side.

I get on, and she gets on behind me, unsure where to put her hands and arms.

"You can put your arms here," I grasp her right arm

with my left hand and pull it around me where her hand is resting close to my dick, "or you can place your arms here. I place her right arm on my waist, higher than the other hand.

"Okay." She wraps her arms around my waist, inches from my zipper.

"Hold on tight. I don't want you falling off." She tightens her hold, her fingers closer to my cock. I clear my throat, attempting to clear my mind to focus on the road.

I start the bike and take off, and the prospect waves us through the gate. We hit the main road and drive away from the club and town. There's nothing except cattle and fields all around us. About five miles from the club, I bought a few hundred acres of land when I first joined the MC. There isn't anything on the land right now, but I rent it out to the rancher who owns the property next to it. I come out here when I need to clear my mind.

The drive comes into view, and I turn down the gravel drive. I come to a stop when the tiny house I had put on the property comes into view, and I turn off my bike, kicking the kickstand down. I help Rosalina off and slide off.

"Where are we?" she asks, looking around.

"My place."

"You live in this tiny house?"

"No." I chuckle. "I come out here when I need some alone time. This would be a good place for us to discuss things. I'll grab some chairs from inside and sit under the trees.

"Okay," she says as she continues to look around.

I get the chairs, and we sit down.

"I'm just going to come out and say this because I don't know how things are done today, but I think you are gorgeous. There is something about you I want. I can't figure it out."

"Yeah. I think you're gorgeous, too." She smiles, then giggles. "You're cute, and you have a nice ass."

A chuckle escapes my lips. "I honestly don't know what to expect from you... I'm older. We didn't do things like ya'll do now, so I'm bound to fuck this up, because they were still passing notes in high school when I graduated. Cellphones were becoming popular if you had the money. First, I want you to call me Ronan. Those close to me call me by my first name." I smile at her, and she smiles back. "So, I have dated no one since my wife." Her smile falls after I mention Kelsey.

"There's a lot I have to tell you. You've met my kids, but I'm sure you've noticed my wife isn't here. A little over eight years ago, she ended her life. After she had Mason, she had postpartum depression. I got her the best care available worldwide and took her to Johns Hopkins and then to Germany. I thought she was doing better, and we returned home. She was gone a week later. I'm not telling you this for your sympathy or anything. I loved my wife, and I haven't been with anyone since her, not even a clubwhore. My kids keep me busy. But then you came into my life. There is something about you that makes me want to take some time out of my day to just talk to you, to be in your presence." I take a breath because I can't believe I'm saying all this shit.

"I think we've established that we like each other or something, and I want to figure out what that is, but I also don't want to piss off your brother. I don't want to ruin our club's relationship because I want to have you in my bed."

She gasps. "Ramiro doesn't have control over who I like and don't like or who I sleep with."

"In this world, he does. So, until I make that call to him, we keep this between me and you."

"It feels like we are sneaking around. Are you embarrassed?"

I stand up, standing in front of her chair, and pull her up into me. Her arms go around my neck.

"Fuck no. I just don't like everyone in my business. That's why I come out here. Everyone is always asking how I'm doing, making sure I'm okay, but I'm good. I'm realizing I'm ready to move on with my life..." I lean down and kiss her, kissing her like I've wanted to the first time I laid eyes on her in the clubhouse. She tastes like everything I've wanted and could never have, but I'm going to have it now.

CHAPTER FIVE

Six Weeks Later

Rosalina

"Lina, help me!" Natalia yells from outside of my room. She has been going nonstop since I asked her to set up the graduation party, which was fine with me because it kept her out of everyone's hair except Warrior's and Tyson's. I'm sure she's been in heaven, but in order for whatever they are planning to work, they have to make sure they have eyes on her at all times.

"Coming!" I yell through the door. Lana and Scarlett are graduating today, and Lana asked me to come, but I told her I was staying back to help with the party. Warrior is going and will record it so I can watch it as we set up.

Something is really off today, and I have a feeling that after tonight, everything is going to change, and there won't be any going back. I'm afraid not so much for Natalia because Warrior has told me some of the information that she has sold to her father's rival gang. I'm so scared for the guys and all those who could be in the crossfire.

They have instructed me to stay away from Natalia when Warrior gets to the party, and I'm to always stick with him because he will keep me safe. Safe from what I've asked him several times, but I don't get an answer, which scares me.

I throw open the door. Natalia is wearing a sheer red dress; you can see through her panties and bra. "Um, isn't that a nightgown?"

"No, it's a beach cover-up. I'm wearing my bikini."

"Oh, they look like your bra and panties."

"I know. That's why I bought it. I'm sure Ty—I'm sure I'll get some guy's attention tonight. I guarantee it." She smiles.

"What do you need help with?"

"Can you help me carry some things to the car? Everything else is at the bar. We have to blow up a lot of balloons."

"Sure." I help her carry a couple of small helium tanks and a few bags of balloons. She's going all out, and I'm sure in her fucked-up head that she's getting brownie points or something for Tyson. I still can't believe I was ever good friends with her.

"Are you riding with me to the bar?"

"No, Warrior is going to drop me off on his way to the graduation ceremony."

"So, what's going on with the two of you?" she asks, then pulls out a compact from her purse to check her makeup.

"We're just talking, getting to know each other. He's had a lot going on in his life."

"No sex yet?"

"No, he's not the fuck 'em and leave 'em type. Warrior isn't who he portrays to be on the outside, and it's refreshing. None of the guys at home can compare to him."

"You staying here, too, then?"

Oh, I hadn't thought about that. I mean, I have, but I haven't. I didn't add in falling hard for Warrior into the equation. "It's possible. I'm sure Ramiro won't like it."

"You're not a child, Lina. You're a woman who can make her own decisions."

"True."

"Damn right, it's true. Gotta fight for what you want, even if someone tries to step in your way." She looks at her phone. "I need to go. See you soon." She gives me a brief hug and gets in her car, quickly driving off.

I just got a pep talk from a psychopath, and I walk into the club, hoping to find Warrior in the common area. He isn't, so I go to his room and knock on the door. The door opens, and my mouth hangs open.

"Oh, hello there." I smile as he is shirtless, and my tongue wants to lick his tattoo all the way to the happy trail that is hidden by his black, tight jeans. Delicious.

"Hey, Lina. Come in, beautiful. I was getting ready to find you so we could leave." He pulls me into his chest, still damp from his shower.

"Perfect timing, then. Natalia left a few minutes ago for Kilkenny's. As far as I can tell, she's all happy about the party."

"I'm sure she is. Please remember, when I get there, do not leave my side. I couldn't stand it if something happened to you…"

"I know, Ronan."

"Mmm, my name off your tongue…" He kisses me, and heat floods my core. If he keeps this up, I'm going to be dripping wet. I end the kiss.

"Keep your thoughts out of the gutter. You have several things that need your attention more than I do." I pull away from him. "Finish getting dressed." I watch him tug on a clean white shirt, tuck it in, and then put on his cut. I swear, some of these guys sleep in their cuts.

"Ready?"

"Yes, we're taking your car, right?" I have a sundress on and don't want to flash everyone.

"I thought I was taking the bike." He winks.

"You would." I shake my head as he grabs his wallet and keys and puts them into his pockets.

"No, I wouldn't. I don't like others seeing what's

mine." His arms wrap around my waist, the heat between us nipping at my exposed flesh.

"I'm yours now?" I look up at him. His eyes are full of mischief.

"Eventually, you will be mine." He kisses my nose, lets go of me, and walks to the door, opening it for me.

"Are you even going to ask me?" I stare him down.

"No. I'll have my answer when I fuck you." He smirks.

"And when will that be?"

"Soon, very soon, because I'm tired of jacking off thinking about you."

I snicker and shake my head. "Tonight?"

"It could be your lucky night."

Finally.

He pulls me out of his room. We have to get going.

"About time you got here," Natalia states as I walk through the bar's doors.

"Sorry, I was waiting on Warrior to get ready. What do you need help with?"

"The rest of the balloons need to be inflated, and we have streamers to tape up."

"I'll get to work on the balloons so when we put the

streamers, we can put up the balloons too, so we aren't doing double the work."

"Sounds good. Thank you for helping. I want to make sure tonight is memorable."

"I'm sure you do." I smile.

When I finish blowing the balloons up, we quickly get them and the streamers in place. Warrior calls me when Scarlett and Lana are getting ready for their pinning ceremony. They have been through a lot and still became registered nurses. It stays a lot about what kind of women they are. The type that I should spend time with.

"Hey, beautiful, we are heading out," Warrior says as he flips the camera around so I can talk to him.

"Okay, be safe. See you soon. Looks like everything's in place."

The next hour goes by in a blur as Natalia has been doing last-minute checks on everything. She's spending a lot of time by the bonfires out back, but I don't know why. At this point, the only thing I understand is what is going on, which is me doing what Warrior asked of me.

Friends and family of Scarlett and Lana trickle in, and so do the guys. The party is ramping up when Warrior walks through the doors. I want to run over and hug him, but I don't know if we are ready for that step. Honestly, I don't give a shit, but I know he does. I respect my brother and all.

He finds his way over and surprises me by taking me in his arms.

"Hi, beautiful." He kisses my forehead.

"Hello, mi amor."

"When are you going to tell me what that means?"

I giggle. "You know what it means. You don't want to admit it yet, and that's okay. We'll get there."

"Are you sure?"

"Oh, yes. I'll tell you later tonight what it means."

"Sounds good. Will you stay with me tonight?"

"Um, the kids?"

"They are far away from the here tonight."

"Your brothers?"

"I'll handle them. I want you in my bed tonight."

"Yes." He kisses me quickly before I can say anything else, and before we can really get into it, he ends the kiss.

"Please remember, don't leave my side, even to go to the restroom. I'll go with you... this isn't up for discussion either."

"Yes, I know. I understand."

"Good. Let's eat."

We get in line to get food, and I see Tyson and Lana come through the door. Lana is looking around, and I notice that she's spotted Natalia. She rolls her eyes, continues looking around, and sees me. She gives me a wave and continues walking through the bar to head out back.

The food was amazing, and the daylight is turning

into nighttime. The guests are leaving and all that's left is club members, ol' ladies, club whores or Chores as Lana calls them, Natalia, and me.

Most of the club members, minus Sledge and Ava, who went back to the club earlier, were sitting around the bonfire. Warrior is holding my hand and rubbing my knuckles. He does it when he is nervous. I'm watching Tyson and Lana in awe of their love for each other, and I hope that Warrior and I head that way. I feel we are.

I look up at Warrior. A chill comes over me, and I feel like I need to get the fuck out of here. I begin to stand, and Warrior yanks me into him as he rolls backward on top of me. The guys shield Lana and me as shots ring out through the darkness.

My ears ring from the sound, and tears fall down my face because I know what I will find when this is all over. Regret fills my body with each shot fired. The pain and agony of losing a so-called friend feels like a knife in the chest.

I can't hear what's happening, but Warrior grabs me, looking me over.

"Are you okay?"

All I can do is nod. I try to work my mouth, but the words won't come out. I can hear sirens in the distance, but they don't sound like normal sirens.

Lana begins to yell at Tyson. "You knew they were coming?"

He doesn't look at her. I can't even stand to look at her.

"Michael Woodford, you tell me the fucking truth," Lana yells.

"Yes, Lana, we knew there was a chance they could come here tonight." He finally looks at her.

"At what cost? How many people are hurt? How many people are dead?" she continues to yell.

"Calm down, Lana. It's under control," Tyson tells her.

"Under control? Look at this place!" she continues.

"The only person who's dead is Natalia," Snaps states as he walks by us. "And some fuckers that shot at us."

"But she's dead!"

"She's dead?" is all I get out. Warrior picks me up and carries me away from the chaos.

"Yes, she's dead, but it's about to get a lot crazier soon. The siren is from the Steel Chains MC, Lana's dad." A bright light shines down on us as a helicopter hovers over us. "We're going after those bastards."

"Okay." My body is numb. I don't know what to think or feel right now.

"Robo will get you to the clubhouse. Go to my room and do not leave there."

I nod.

"You'll be okay, beautiful. We will get everything worked out."

Gunfire rings out in the distance, causing me to jump.

"It means my love."

"What does?"

"Mi amor. My love. Please be careful." I kiss his cheek. I look around, and Robo's close by, waiting for Warrior to release me to his care. "I'll see you later."

I walk with Robo to his truck, which looks like an old tank.

"Thank you," I tell him as he opens my door.

"Warrior would kick my ass if I didn't show his ol' lady some respect." He winks and closes the door, then gets in.

My brain is on overload… Natalia is dead, but Warrior wants to claim me… as his ol' lady. I close my eyes. If I drift off, Robo will wake me up when we get there.

CHAPTER
SIX

Warrior

Watching her walk away with another man kills me, even though I know he would die in order to keep her safe. Not only because she's Jaguar's sister, but because she's mine.

"Are you going chopper?" Snaps asks as the blades whirl above us, and a ladder comes down from the bay.

"No, you go with VPeep and Cash. I will stay here with Tyson and take care of the bodies."

He nods. "Be prepared. They might come back here if we get them cornered."

"That's what we planned," I say as VPeep and Cash walk over.

I steady the ladder, allowing my brothers to get up to the helicopter, and the ladder pulls up as they go up and out of sight. I roll my neck, trying to relieve some of the tension that's been collecting since I called Jaguar this morning.

I heard his threats of gutting me and leaving me to die in the desert loud and clear if I hurt his sister, but I put that to the back of my mind for now. I pull out my phone, needing to call Sledge to complete what we're doing with Natalia's body, and press send.

"Everything went as planned?"

"Yes, Prez. The Ivory Wolves shot up the wrong place, and we got a few of them. Slasher's group came in with a chopper, and they were up in the sky working on cornering them with their crew on the ground. VPeep, Snaps, and Cash are with them."

"All the ol' ladies out of there?"

I look around and see June, Lana, and Scarlett are still around. None of the club whores were in sight.

"No, I'll work on that now. What do you want me to do with Natalia's body?"

"Wrap her up. We need to get her to Mexico. Alvarez wants her buried there."

"Would be better to dump her body in the Gulf."

"Na, that would pollute the water." He chuckles.

"I'll get everything here tidied up."

"Call if anything changes." He hangs up.

"June?" I call out as I walk toward her, and she looks over to me and meets me halfway.

"Take my car and get Lana and Scarlett out of here."

"Lana doesn't want to leave Tyson."

"Okay, I'll talk to her." I walk over to where she's up Tyson's ass, and I know this will not be easy.

"Lana?"

"What?" she snaps.

"You need to go to the clubhouse with June." I'm trying to stay calm, but they need to get out of here.

"I'm not leaving Tyson," Lana states.

Who is this person, and where did Lana go? I grab ahold of her shoulders, making her look at me. "This isn't up for discussion. You need to go to the clubhouse now. Tyson will be there in a bit," I grit out.

"No." She stands tall.

"You're acting like a fucking spoiled princess." I pick her up, and she hits my back. Why Tyson couldn't do this is beyond me. "June, Scarlett, let's go." They follow me to my car, and I place Lana in the front seat. "Go to the fucking clubhouse and stay there. Don't fuck with me on this. Your ol' man should put you in your place, but right now, he's focused on keeping the club safe, not just you. So, grow the fuck up." She gulps as I slam the door, not allowing her to say anything.

"June?"

"Yes?" she asks as I open the car door for her.

"Check on Lina for me, please."

"Will do. Make sure my ol' man comes back to us."

I nod my head, then shut the door.

The engine revs to life, and she spins out as she pops it into second gear instead of first as she takes off. At least she can drive a manual. I look around after I watch the car drive off. There are a few bodies from where they were shooting from the bed of a truck. The prospects can get this cleaned up and dispose of the bodies.

I go inside the bar, looking for something to wrap Natalia in so I can transport her to the club. There's a tablecloth, and I take it outside and take a shuddering breath as I know this will fuck with my head. I roll her over, and the shot is through the heart. I get blood on my hands, and I freeze.

"Kelsey, don't leave me... don't leave us. We need you," I shout as I watch the life fade from her body.

"Goodbye, Ron, I love yo..." she's unable to finish the last word. I wrap her arm with towels and her body with a blanket and run to Alvarez's room.

"Help, I need help!" I yell. The guys come out of their rooms, and Alvarez opens the door.

"Put her on my bed. How long ago did you find her?"

"Five minutes ago."

He checks for a pulse. "I don't know if I can do anything," he says as he removes the towel drenched her in blood and places it back on her arm.

Alvarez opens his bag on the desk and pulls out vials and bottles. He quickly gets to work on closing the gash in her arm as he attempts to revive her.

Everything is a blur, and I don't understand what's happening. My brothers surround me, and I collapse. The weight of everything's too much, and I crumble under the pressure.

"I'm sorry, Warrior, but she lost too much blood from the severed artery. I tried to repair it, but I'm sorry, she's gone."

"She's dead?" falls from my mouth. *"No, she can't be dead. She can't leave me. I need her," I cry out.*

"She's dead," echoes in my ears as Lina says it over and over. I need to make sure she's okay. She knew how evil Natalia was, but that doesn't mean it didn't hurt any less. Natalia was her friend… a friend who deceived the club.

I continue to wrap her body in the cheap piece of material fitting for her, and once I'm done, I leave her there for a prospect to move her when the van is ready.

"We got them." Snaps voice comes through the phone. "We captured three of them, and Slasher said they would take care of them."

"Everything is about clean here. Natalia's body is in Pappy's van on ice."

"See you at the club," he says as he ends the call.

"Tyson, ready to head back?"

"Yeah," he says as he looks at his phone. "Hey, thanks for handling Lana. She wasn't listening to me because she was in shock or something."

"We protect our own, bro."

"They're bringing back three?"

"Yeah. Put them in the shed and let Steel Chains deal with them."

"I'm going to make sure I get a piece of them," he grits.

"It's a good bonding experience with your future father-in-law." I chuckle.

"Damn right." He smiles. "You riding with me?"

"Yeah. June hot rodded my car."

"Oh, Cash is going to be in trouble because she'll want one, too."

"It won't fit all their kids."

"That's the point." He laughs as we walk to his truck. I get in, and *'she's dead'* still echoes in the back of my mind.

My mind is calm when we pull through the gates of the club. He parks the truck, and we get out. Sledge meets us at the front of the clubhouse.

"Church in twenty," he states.

"Yes, Prez," we say in unison. I have enough time to run upstairs to see Lina and change my clothes. Tyson and I walk through the club. Even though he has a house off-property, he keeps a room for her in case of shit like this. I follow behind him as he takes the steps two at a time, wanting to get to his woman, and I do the same because it feels like it's been months since I've seen Rosalina.

I turn right down the hallway and enter my room quietly. She's probably sleeping, and I don't want to wake her if she is.

"Ronan?" her soft voice stills me.

"Yes, beautiful," I say as I turn on the lamp and sit on the edge of the bed.

"Hold me," she murmurs as tears trickle down her cheek.

Screw changing clothes. I kick off my boots and lay next to her, pulling her into my arms.

"What's going to happen to Natalia's body?" she asks as she snuggles her face into the crook of my neck.

"I don't have all the details, but she's returning to Mexico."

"I want to go. I-I need closure."

"I'll go with you."

"Okay…"

"We have church, so I have to get going, but I'll be back up here as soon as we're finished, okay?"

She nods and holds me tighter.

"Do you want me to leave the light on?" I ask, and she knows I have to get going and releases her hold on me.

"Yes, please."

"I'll be back soon, beautiful." I kiss her on the lips, and her hand cups my face.

"Mi amor." She gives me a small smile, and I take her hand from my face, kiss her palm, and then place it on the bed.

I leave the room, even though I want to stay there and have my way with her. It's been so long. When we finally have sex, I'll last only two minutes.

The room was almost full when I arrived. I sit next to Tyson and Lana, who gives me a side-eye look as I sit down. Snaps and Preach sit on the other side of me, and VPeep walks in, taking the last seat on the board so the meeting can start.

"I called this meeting because a lot has happened in the past six hours. As you know, Alvarez and Jaguar confirmed that Natalia Alvarez sold intel to the Ivory Wolves MC on Lana. We put a plan in motion to set a trap for Natalia and the Ivory Wolves. That plan was executed tonight. From the reports I've received, the mission was successful. Tyson, your report."

"Natalia had set up the party for everyone to be inside the bar at twenty-two hundred hours, and we confirmed that is the intel she gave the Ivory Wolves. Instead, we set up bonfires outside to hide our positions and blocked Natalia's phone from calling in or out. She was trying to get Lana's attention when the first shots rang out. With our position, we killed several in the back of the truck, along with Natalia. Steel Chains MC sounded a siren when they were in position, causing the Ivory Wolves to move out right into the trap we set for them. The helicopter came in, taking VPeep, Snaps, and Cash up in the air to help track and take out rival gang members. Two hours later, all but three Ivory Wolves members are deceased. The three we captured are in the shed, and Slasher and his members are handling business," Tyson states.

"Do we know if the Ivory Wolves were working with anyone else?" Sledge asks as he looks at Robo.

"They have been in contact with the Cartel, but I have seen nothing come through where they are working on a deal or asking for support," he responds after reviewing his notes.

"The Ivory Wolves were not our rival, but they came on our turf to take down one of our own. From here on out, they are our enemy. You are to kill on sight. Ask questions later. If they have an in with the Cartel, then they know where we are. The club is on lockdown until we know what's happening in Mexico. Everyone clear on that." He looks right at Lana, and she lowers her chin. I'm sure he heard about how she was acting.

"Yes, Prez," echoes through the room.

"Good. Next business. I need someone to take Natalia's body to Mexico."

"I'll do it. Rosalina wants to be there for the funeral."

"I'll send Pappy with you."

"Yes, Prez."

"Head out after you get some sleep. Wolf, Lucky, Raider, and Wardog, two on and two off. When we adjourn, one of you go with Wolf."

"I will, Prez," Raider states.

"Thanks, brother. Anything else?" He waits for a moment. "Adjourned. Get some rest."

I stand and turn to walk out.

"Warrior," Sledge calls from behind me.

I turn around.

"Make sure you see me before you leave. I have Robo working on some tech for you to take with you for Diablo."

"Yes, sir."

I leave the room and make my way upstairs. Exhaustion hits my body, and as much as I want to claim Rosalina as mine, it will have to wait. I discard my clothes and crawl into bed, hoping not to wake her. Her soft breathing tells me I accomplished my goal, and it pulls me asleep.

CHAPTER
SEVEN

Rosalina

I feel like I'm in an oven, and it feels good. It's better than waking up cold. I open my eyes, and Ronan's arms are wrapped around me, holding me close. I take a deep breath; I can't believe I'm here with him. He's been all about taking it slow, getting to know each other, and making sure that this is what we want. Yes, he's old-fashioned, but it's cute, and I feel valued. Most guys just want a piece of ass, then they are done with you. That isn't the feeling that I'm getting with Ronan at all. It's like he's savoring every bit of me, piece by piece. I believe he wants to make sure that I don't feel like he is taking advantage of me since he's older. The age difference bothers him slightly, but he's working on it.

"Do you always think this much when you wake up?" he mumbles into my hair.

"How did you know I was thinking?"

"Your head slightly moves left to right as you work through whatever you're thinking." He caresses my back with his fingers, sending warmth throughout my body. I snuggle into him more.

"Oh, it does not." Maybe it does, now that I think about it.

"And you bite your lip, and I can feel your chin moving since it's resting on my chest."

"Are you always so perceptive?" I pull my head back to look at his face. His chiseled face is covered with brown whiskers with a sprinkling of gray, and his brown hair is short, high, and tight military cut with silver streaks. Looking at him without his cut, he doesn't look like he's in an MC. Ronan looks like he is ready to fight another war, but not for his country, for his brotherhood.

"Yes, because the lives of my brothers and children depend on it." He looks at me and winks.

"I take it you're not a morning person?"

He chuckles. "I've only been asleep for," he pulls his arm out from around me and looks at his wrist, "two and a half hours."

"I'm sorry I woke you up."

He pulls me back into his chest, and I sigh because I never want to leave this moment.

"It's okay. I have a lot to do today… including you."

"Oh, me? I'm excited to be on your list."

"You have been for a while."

"Are we going to talk about what happened last night?"

"Not right now. What I'm going to do now is help you get out of your clothes and show me what I've been missing out on over the past couple of months. If you want to."

"What are you waiting for? It will be faster if you help me." I giggle as his hands find the hem of my shirt and help pull it over my head. The only thing between him and me is my panties. He rubs his hand down the lacy material, pressing along my slit. Ronan stops, then tugs the thin material down my legs. My body is fully accessible to him.

He stands up and pushes his boxer down, his erection on full display. Ronan gets back on the bed, crawling up my body, kissing my thigh as he goes.

"Spread your legs," he commands. I hesitate. "Rosalina, do you not want me to touch you?"

"Yes, I want to do this with you."

"Then spread your legs…"

I comply, and he doesn't waste any time. Ronan licks my slit, then pushes a finger in and out of me as his other hand rubs my clit. I moan, closing my eyes as my hands bunch up the sheets on the bed. He adds another finger, and he roughly fucks with his fingers. My orgasm is building quickly, and I moan out as I'm falling over the edge, coming all over his hands. He doesn't stop. Ronan keeps the steady pace of in and out, in and out, while rubbing my clit. I didn't think I could have back-to-back orgasms, but my body tightened with another one.

Ronan continues until I scream out his name, and he removes his fingers and licks the juices off.

"Mmm…" He leans down and kisses me, and it's intoxicating to taste me on his tongue.

He leans over and opens the nightstand drawer, pulls out a condom, and quickly sheaths his cock.

"Sorry, beautiful. This is going to be fast and rough."

Ronan slams himself into my center, and waves of pleasure go throughout my body. His cock hits all the right places, and I feel another orgasm building. But I don't know if I can find my release.

"Come, beautiful. You're clamping down on me. I can't hold out much longer," he grits out.

He leans back and puts his thumb on my clit, and rubs it, pushing me over the edge.

"Oh, Ronan," is all I can say as he mumbles my name as he finds his release, then slowly pulls out of me. A few moments pass as we catch our breath. He gets out of bed and goes into the bathroom. The shower turns on, and he returns to the room with a washcloth and cleans me. That's a first.

"Fuck, babe," he says as he leans over and kisses me. "I don't know if I'll ever last over two minutes with you."

"Is that a compliment?"

"Yes." He chuckles. "Shower with me?"

"Yes, I would love that."

Ronan gets off the bed and waits for me to sit up. He offers me his hand and pulls me into him from the bed. I've never been this exposed to a man before, but I know I'm safe, and I feel myself falling for him more and more, even though it's only been a few months.

I step into the steamy shower, and he steps in behind me.

"May I wash you?"

"Only if I can return the favor."

He smiles and nods and grabs a washcloth from the ledge. Ronan wets the cloth and pours body wash on.

"Sorry, it's a guy scent… You're the only woman I've showered with…" he says the last part quietly. I don't question him. I close my eyes and let him do whatever he wants.

After our long shower, we take a nap and wake up feeling refreshed. Ronan shows me the difference between sex and fucking. The first time we had sex, it was a slow burn that had me slowly climbing to my orgasm. But this time, we fucked fast, hot, raw emotions that had me coming before I knew what hit me. This is a huge perk of being with someone who's older. They know how to please a woman.

"Everything okay?" Ronan asks as he brings me a glass of water.

"Yes." I smile and take a sip of water.

"You were chewing on that lip pretty good. Regretting being here with me?"

"Fuck no," I shout. "Oops, sorry. No, I don't regret being with you. Whatever this is between you and me, I want it. I want more of it as long as I can get it."

"My age doesn't bother you?" he asks as he sits on the edge of the bed.

"No, if anything, I find it more attractive. You haven't rushed or pressured me into anything. You've taken the time to get to know me instead of trying to woo me into your bed. It's taken us over three months to get here, but it was so worth the wait." I pull him down and kiss him.

"What happened to the shy Rosalina that came to the club?"

I snicker. "I'll blame that on being around Savannah and Lana."

"That will do it." He lays down beside me. "So, you ready to hear the details?"

"No, but tell me, anyway."

"Natalia is dead, and we are taking her back to Mexico tonight. Pappy is going with us, and we're taking his van."

"Tonight?"

"Yes, so we need to get up and get ready to go soon. The prospects packed up Natalia's belongings in her room. Did you have anything in there?"

"No."

"I also had them pack up your room…"

"Why?"

"Because I would like you to move into my room when we get back from Mexico." He looks me in the eyes, searching for a hint of regret. I regret he won't find it because there isn't any.

"Oh," I breathe out. Holy shit. "What about the kids?"

"We will talk to them together. They both like you, so it shouldn't be an issue."

"Yes, I'll stay with you."

"Good, because I want access to you whenever I want." He kisses my nose, and I love it.

"Do I get the same privilege?" I smirk.

"Absolutely, beautiful. I'm yours anytime you want me."

"How about now?"

"You drive a hard bargain but sold." He stands, removing the shorts that he put on to get to the kitchen for water. "Get on your knees, beautiful. I'm going to fuck you from behind."

I do as he instructs, and Ronan takes his cock and teases my slit, aligning himself with my center. He grasps my hips and thrusts inside of me.

"This is going to be rough and quick. Touch

yourself, play with your clit, beautiful." I move my hand between my legs to my clit and flick it, causing my orgasm to climax quickly with each thrust of his cock. I rub and flick, climbing higher and high, and I explode on his dick as he yells out my name. I collapse on the bed and fall asleep. For our trip, I need to rest.

CHAPTER
EIGHT

Warrior

Once I hear Rosalina softly breathing, I get out of bed so she can sleep. I don't know if I'll ever be able to get enough of her. Intellectually, she's smart and has thoughts that differ from my own. I forget that she's twenty-four to my thirty-eight. She's closer to Madison's age than my own, and at first, it fucked with my head because I thought maybe she had some kind of daddy issues... If she does, she hides it well.

I know she's torn about going home because it will make everything that happened with Natalia real. Rosalina told me that Natalia was the first friend she made when they moved to Mexico, so she's going to be in her head when she gets back, especially if something triggers memories. I hope she will want to come back to Texas. Mexico has been her home for the past six years, and I don't want to force her to choose her home or me.

As I make my way downstairs, I look at my watch. It's not even noon yet. It feels like the day should be almost over. I make my way to Sledge's office and knock on the door.

"Come in," he hollers.

I open the door, walk in, and shut it behind me. "You wanted me to come and see you before I left?"

"Yea, Robo has the tech for BCMC Mexico. He has it in his office, so stop by there and get it."

"Yes, Prez. I will."

"How's it going with Rosalina?"

"Good..."

"You don't seem so sure."

"I'm sure. I just don't want to hurt her or get hurt."

"Women are tricky, you know that."

"That's what I'm afraid of."

"A few days in Mexico should be good for the both of you. Help her decide if what she wants is here or if it's in Mexico."

"I talked to Jaguar. He didn't have any issues with me claiming her as my ol' lady, but he told me if I hurt her, he would kill me. I don't doubt him for a second."

He chuckles. "He's a feisty fucker, which is why he's the VP. Still heading out at twenty hundred hours?"

"That's the plan. Pappy and Rosalina are sleeping now. I'm going to take a nap in a bit after I know everything is packed."

"The prospects loaded everything to conceal the body in case you're stopped, but you shouldn't have any issues since we verified a few agents on our payroll are working today."

"Good to know."

"Be safe, brother."

"Will do."

I leave his office and go to the kitchen to make a sandwich. It must be a lazy Sunday because no one is in here. I pull everything I need from the fridge, place it on the counter, and then grab a plate from the cabinet. The kitchen door opens, and I turn around. Lana stands on the other side of the table, looking like she's at a loss for words.

"Hey, Lana," I simply state.

"Hi," she replies. I guess she isn't very talkative today.

"Have you seen your father yet?" I hadn't seen any of the guys from Steel Chains MC, but they are staying in our guest building, which is a smaller version of the clubhouse.

"Yes, I just came from talking to him. I hadn't seen him in so long..."

"I'm sure he is proud of you."

"He is... Um, about last night—"

"Don't worry about it. I know that wasn't really you. You're safe, and that's what matters."

"I'm sorry, though. I should have listened to Tyson."

"Apology accepted. Now, don't worry about it anymore, okay?"

"Yeah." She gives me a small smile. "Do you need help with the kids while you're in Mexico?"

"I think June has it under control but take them for a day or so to give her a break. I don't plan on being gone longer than a week."

"I'll check in with her."

"Thank you. Want a sandwich?"

"I'm good, thanks, though. Might want to make one for Lina." She winks, turns, and leaves the kitchen.

That's probably not a bad idea. After making a second sandwich, I put everything back up. I grab a couple of pops from the fridge and a bag of chips from the pantry and take everything upstairs. I probably should wake her up so we can get her bags packed, and the kids picked up so we can spend time together before we leave.

Rosalina was awake when I went upstairs, and she inhaled the sandwich I made for her and some of mine. She isn't shy about eating like some women. I gave her some of my clothes to wear over to the room she was staying in so she could change and pack what she wanted to take with her, and the rest would get moved into my room while we were gone.

"I need to get my things so you can spend time with the kids before we go," Rosalina states as she puts her flip-flops on and sits on the edge of the bed.

"You're not going to spend time with them, too?"

"I will not intrude, Ronan. You've missed a lot of time with them lately, and we're going to be gone five or six days."

I pull her up from the bed and into a kiss, and she melts into me. "What are you going to do?"

"I'll probably find Savannah or Lana and chat with them for a while."

"Sounds good. Let's get your clothes."

We walk hand in hand down the stairs and through the clubhouse. The common room is full since we are on lockdown. We step outside and into the dorm building. Slasher sits on the couch, talking to one of his members as we walk through.

"Hey, Slasher."

"Warrior. Thanks for taking care of my girl last night. She's hardheaded like her ol' man."

"Which one?" We laugh.

"Be careful in Mexico. There are rumblings that the Ivory Wolves are working with the cartel. The cartel is everywhere down there."

"That's what I've been told. I plan on getting down there and getting back." Rosalina's hand tenses in mine.

"Slasher, this is Rosalina Rodrígues, she's Jaguar's sister."

"Nice to meet you. I'm Lana's father."

"Nice to meet you too, sir." Her voice is soft.

"We'll let you get back to what you were doing. I need to get the last few things in order to leave soon."

"Stay safe, brother." He offers his hand, and I shake it, knowing I would disrespect him if I didn't.

"Likewise." I grab Rosalina's hand again and walk to her room. We enter, and someone has neatly boxed everything with labels.

"This box says clothes," I point out.

"Let's look at that one."

I open the box, and she goes through it. "I will not bring a lot because I still have a lot of clothes at home."

"That works. Do you have everything you need, then?"

"I need my makeup and bathroom stuff."

We looked through other boxes and found one labeled bathroom.

"Try this one." I open it, and she looks in it, pulling bag after bag of stuff out. "You don't use all of that, do you?"

"Yes, every day. I have a routine for the morning and evening."

"I don't know if there's enough room in my bathroom."

"I'll make room, don't you worry. You don't need ten rolls of half used toilet paper…"

"Those are my emergency rolls." I smile.

"Seriously? They are taking up space."

"They are not." I put the box lid down and began to tickle her.

"Ronan, stop!" She giggles. "I'm extremely ticklish. Oh my God. Please, stapppp!" She continues to laugh. I grab her by the waist, pick her up, and carry her to the bed. I lay her down and crawl up her body.

"I'm going to miss you."

"You'll be fine, I promise. Spend time with the kids. Sneak in getting some ice cream while you're out and make them happy. Then, when you're ready to go, I'll be ready."

"That's a good idea. You know what another good idea is?"

"What?"

"Getting you out of those clothes and letting me bury myself inside of you."

"You're insatiable."

"Yes, I am. I've had a taste of you, and I want more." I caress her body, pushing the hem of the shirt over her chest, exposing her lacy bra, and over her head. I know she doesn't have any panties on, so the only thing between me and her core is basketball shorts.

I quickly tug them down and off her body.

I lick my lips as I unzip my pants and push them down, releasing my erection. Fucking her is mind-blowing, and I can't wait to blow my load inside of her.

It's going to be quick, but at least I know it will be good.

CHAPTER
NINE

Rosalina

I watch Ronan leave to pick up the kids, and I walk back into the clubhouse to find Savannah. She and Phoebe are sitting on the couch watching TV. The room has cleared out since earlier.

"Hey, can I join you?"

"Have you ever seen *Steel Magnolias?*" Savannah asks as she turns back toward the TV.

"I don't think so…"

"Oh, my God. Sit your ass down and grab some tissues. You'll need them by the time it's over."

"Where did everyone go?"

"They cleared out when this came on. It's a tearjerker, and I've made them watch it. I don't know how many times." She snickers. "Just because they are in an MC doesn't mean they can't be cultured in film."

"How old is it?"

"Older than me, but not as old as my brother."

"Which is?"

"Thirty-five, and I'm twenty-nine."

"I didn't realize that you were older than me."

"Just a little... oh, this is a good part."

She grabs popcorn and shoves it in her mouth. The women work in a hair salon and all the gossip that goes along with that. The movie pulls me in, and I bawl at the end when Shelby dies. Ouiser was definitely my favorite character. Spunky old woman who kind of reminds me of my mom.

I haven't talked to her much since I've been here. I should call and tell her I'm going back to Mexico. She will worry.

"Thanks for letting me join you guys. I'll see you when I get back."

"Safe travels, girl." She stands and hugs me.

"See you later, Lina," Phoebe responds. She's always so quiet.

"Bye."

I run upstairs to Ronan's room and make sure I shut the door behind me. Getting my phone out of my back pocket, I hit call when my mom's name appeared in my favorite contacts.

"Hello," my mother's voice echoes through the phone. Hmm. Someone is listening to our call. Usually, there isn't anything wrong with our calls, and Ramiro made sure I learned to listen for weird things on phone calls.

"Hey, Mom. Just calling to check in. How are you?"

"I'm doing well. The snow is off the mountain." That's our code word for we're being listened to. The snow doesn't disappear until June... and if it is gone, then we say the opposite.

"Must be pretty warm there."

"Stifling."

"Talk care of yourself, Mama. When Ramiro gets home, I'll let him know we've talked." Meaning, I'll let someone know that they bugged our phones.

"Sounds good. I love you."

"I love you too, Mama." I hang up the phone. I don't know which phone is tapped, but I shut mine off and head downstairs.

Sledge is walking down the hallway, and I get his attention.

"Hey, Prez," I call out.

He stops and turns around. "What's up, Rosalina?"

"I was talking to my mom, and we were pretty sure someone tapped it."

"Did you give out any information?"

"No, when she started talking, it was echoed and delayed. We both knew what was going on, and she code-worded me to keep it basic. I turned my phone off as soon as I hung up with her."

"Good girl. I'm sure Jaguar has it where all your locations are off and everything."

"Yes, I don't mess with anything on my phone except to add contacts."

"I'll have Robo check it out and see what he can find. Can I take your phone?"

"Of course." I hand him my phone, and he gently takes it from me.

"Thanks. I'll get it back to you before you leave." He turns to head down the hallway.

"Thank you."

"You're welcome."

I hear the door open and see Mason and Madison walk through. They see me and run over to me.

"Dad told us you're like his girlfriend!" Mason shouts.

"Calm down, Mason," Madison states. "So, is it true?" she asks me.

I look up at Ronan, and he's grinning.

"Couldn't wait?" I smile.

"Nope."

"Yes, if that is what your dad called me, then that's what I am."

"Good! I like you. You're a lot cooler than Dad," Madison breathes out.

"So, are you going to be kissing Dad and stuff? Ew," Mason says as he makes a disgusted face.

"I won't do anything that would embarrass you... I'll make sure that your dad does the same, okay?"

"Thank you," they say in unison.

"Do you want to hang out with us before you leave?

Dad said that you're going home for a few days," Madison asks.

"Yes, I'm going to see my brother. I kind of miss him."

"I would be excited to get away from my brother," Madison states as she rolls her eyes.

"You'd miss him after a while, though." I smile. "What are you going to do?"

"Play air hockey and eat junk food!" Mason adds.

"Oh, count me in."

"You go ahead, and I'll grab the food," Ronan states, pulling me to the side. "Thanks for hanging out. They were excited when I told them about us."

"That's sweet and absolutely. It will be fun."

We played air hockey for over two hours and almost ate the kitchen out of junk food. I feel sorry for whoever is picking up groceries this week. The kids who swore they would still be wound up at 8 p.m., but they both passed out a little after 7. Ronan tucked them both in and made sure June was aware of everything that was going on over the next week.

"Ready?" Ronan asks as he walks through the common room.

"I need to get my phone from Robo. Hopefully, he could figure out what was going on."

"If he hasn't by now, he will shortly. I'll be right back."

Robo's office is off-limits to non-members, so I make sure I have my purse, passport, and everything else I might need.

After twenty minutes, Ronan returns with a box and hands me my phone.

"He hit dead ends with your phone, but he can see where they were. Might be a good idea to get a new phone and phone number while we are in Mexico."

"I agree."

"Pappy is waiting for us outside."

I nod, and he takes my hand after I put my phone in my purse. He opens the door to the van, and there is a pillow and blanket on the seat. He knew I would probably sleep. I look behind the seat, and there is a panel, so I can't see what's back there, but I know what's back there. I hope no one asks.

He helps me into the van and shuts the door, and Ronan gets in the passenger seat, as Pappy is already in the front seat. Even though the van looks like a pedo van from the outside, there are windows inside that you can see out of. I watch as the scenery passes us by.

My surroundings look less familiar as we head southwest, and my eyes get heavier and heavier as time passes. Before I realize it, I'm falling asleep thinking about how I will tell my brother that I've fallen in love with Ronan.

CHAPTER
TEN

Warrior

I knew the drive would be long, but it was even more stressful in a different country. We've stopped a few times to stretch, get gas, and get something to eat. The sun is beginning to peak over the horizon, so we are getting close. This terrain is unfamiliar, but it's not too different from home. Only one road, 180, will take you to Tampico, and it's full of little villages and towns along the way.

GPS states that we'll be there soon, and I can't wait to get out of this van and into bed. I do not know if Jaguar will allow me to sleep with Rosalina. Although I told him my intentions, I don't want to disrespect him in his home.

I lean back and attempt to wake Rosalina. "Hey,

beautiful. You're almost home." After I said you were home, I felt like I smashed my nuts. I want her home to be with me. There could be a chance that she would want to stay here now that she's back. I have to show her I want her with me. The kids want her in their lives, too.

She stirs awake.

"Hey, good morning." She smiles.

"Hi." I wink. "We're almost at the clubhouse in Tampico."

"Already?" She bolts upright in the seat.

"Yes, you slept the entire time."

"I didn't mean to." She rubs her eyes, trying to wake up.

"It's okay.

Rosalina looks around and looks as if she's about to cry.

"Are you okay?"

"Yeah... See that house over there?" She points at a two-story house that's out of place. It's been taken care of; it's high dollar and doesn't fit in the area.

"Yes, what about it?"

"That's Natalia's mom's house. She stayed there when she wasn't staying with me."

Alvarez paid for that house. "You live in the clubhouse?"

"Yes, I do. Remember, Ramiro likes to babysit me... turn right here. It's tricky, and GPS always messes it up. I think someone messed it up on purpose."

"Right there?" Pappy points at a gravel drive between two closed businesses.

"Yes, right there."

He turns down the drive.

"The club owns all of this property. The repair shop is a legitimate business, and they are working on getting a few more club businesses up and going. They bought out the area so no one would snoop around the club."

"Smart idea. That's what they did with our club. We have a three-decade history in our club."

"Isn't that unusual?"

"It depends. Some of the bigger gangs have been around since the 1930s."

We pull up to a barbed wire fence gate.

"Indique su negocio."

"Héctor, déjanos entrar," Rosalina states as she sticks her head between the seats.

"Señorita Rosalina, le esperan. Entrar." He rushes out and opens the gate for us.

"Seems like he's afraid of you."

"Yes, most of the guys are. They know if anything happens to me, Jaguar will kill whoever fucked up."

"I think your brother and I will get along just fine."

"Me, too." She smiles.

Buildings appear, and they look nothing like ours. The most prominent building is three stories tall, and palm trees flank the front.

"That's the clubhouse. The building to the right is

the whorehouse and where the guests stay. Warrior, you're not staying there. Pappy can have enough fun for both of you."

"Um, yes, ma'am." I wink at her.

"That is the clinic that Alvarez works out of, but he is training a new doctor since he has the facility that Tyson was in."

We pull up in front of the clubhouse, and several men stand outside. I open the door and get out, and then open the door for Rosalina to get out.

"Rosie!" a guy yells, approaches and hugs her.

"Ramiro, I've missed you."

"I've missed you, too, but you've been a valuable asset to the clubs."

"I tried to be." She smiles.

"Warrior," he offers his hand to shake, and I take it, "it's nice to finally meet you in person. We have a lot to talk about."

"Yes, we do."

"I'll introduce you to everyone else. This is Diablo, our prez, and his wife Maria, and of course you know Alvarez. The others are prospects, and the rest you'll meet at Church."

"Nice to meet you both, and Alvarez. It's good to see you, doctor. This is Pappy," I point to him standing quietly by the van, and he waves."

"Hello. It's good to see you, too, young man. Keeping those kids in line?"

"Absolutely."

"Thank you for bringing her home." Alvarez looks like he's aged a lot since he left Texas.

"Anything for you. Do you need help with anything?"

"No, we have it covered. Rosalina can show you where you are staying, and I'll have a prospect show Pappy to his room. We'll let you rest, then have Church at two."

"Thank you. Talk soon." I grab our bags from the van and am relieved I get to sleep with Rosalina after all. My cock stirs to life. But right now, all I want is some sleep. She guides me through the clubhouse, and I will not remember where anything is until I see it again.

We climb the stairs to the third floor.

"I'm the only one up here. The Prez and his wife live in a house on the back side of the property, and the rest of the voted-in members sleep on the second floor."

"So, we have privacy?"

"Yes." She grins.

"It's going to have to wait because I need sleep."

"I'll snuggle with you," she says as he opens the door to her room. Sunlight filters through the curtains, illuminating the space. They modernly decorated the room with a queen-sized bed in the center. I drop the bags, take my cut off, place it on the chair, strip down to my boxers, and fall into bed.

My eyes close before I hit the pillow, and I'm out.

I jolt out of bed as a nightmare rips through my dream, and I rub my eyes to get the picture out of my mind. The space beside me is cold, and the room is unfamiliar. Once I get my bearings, I remember I'm in Mexico. Rosalina is probably with Jaguar. I take a few deep breaths to calm my racing heart. Usually, it's Kelsey I see dying in my dreams, but this time, it was Rosalina, and they shot her. I lie back in bed and tell myself that the lack of sleep is fucking with my head.

The door opens, and Rosalina comes into the room.

"I was hoping to come and wake you up." She smirks and crawls into bed. "Oh, what's wrong?"

"Nothing. Just trying to wake up." I wrap my arms around her and pull her into my chest.

"The ladies have been cooking since yesterday. After you meet with Jaguar, dinner will be ready."

"Good, I'm starving, but I need to shower before Church."

"I will show you where everything is. I wish I could join you, but if I don't return soon, I know Ramiro will come looking for me." She giggles. "He's already trying to mother me.

"That's what big brothers are for."

"I guess, but he's a pain in my ass," she says as she unwraps herself from my hold. "You should get going. They called for Church to start an hour before I came here."

"Fuck. Okay."

She gets off the bed, and I sit up, stretching my stiff body. I look where I dropped our bags, and they weren't there.

"Where's my bag?"

"I put it in the bathroom. I figured you would need it in there."

"Thanks."

She walks over to the opposite side of the room and flips on the light. "Here's the bathroom. There is a towel out for you already."

"Are you sure you don't want to shower with me?"

"It's super tempting, but I don't know how Ramiro would react..."

"I know, I'm teasing you. Give me ten minutes, and I'll be ready to head downstairs."

"Okay. I'll wait."

I walk into the bathroom, and there are makeup products everywhere... this is what I have to look forward to when we get back. I'm going to have to find us a house to have room in, or maybe build one. I turn the shower on and let it get hot. I get in and let the water cascade down my back for a few minutes, then wash my hair and body. Once I feel clean, I rinse off and turn the water off. I grab the towel and dry off. Five minutes later, I walk out to put my cut on.

"I had to stop myself from coming in there," Rosalina says, getting up from the chair and hands me my cut.

"I wish you would have," I say, putting my cut on.

"You can show me tonight how much you missed me taking a shower with you." She smiles as she leans into me, then kisses my cheek. "Ready?"

"Yes." I wrap my arms around her and grab her ass, pulling her into me. "This should tell you how much I missed you," I say as I grind my cock into her stomach.

She bites her lip. "We better go before we go too far…"

"Yeah," I breathe out.

I let go of her ass but grab her hand as I leave the room because I want it known that I'm claiming Rosalina as mine. As we approach the main floor, Jaguar is leaning on the back of the couch.

"I was about to come and get you." He shoots daggers in my direction.

"Sorry, I slept a little longer than I wanted to." I smirk.

"This way to the sanctuary." He stands from the couch and walks away, leaving me behind.

I look at Rosalina, who's blushing. "I'll see you soon, beautiful." I kiss her cheek and walk in the direction Jaguar is headed.

He's waiting for me by the door, not looking too happy. I get there, he walks in, and I follow him in. I sit in the back since I'm from another chapter.

The gavel sounds. Church is in session.

CHAPTER **ELEVEN**

Rosalina

It feels like the guys have been in Church forever, but I know it hasn't been that long. I lie on the couch and turn on the TV. There is a lot to do. Even though Natalia was a traitor, we are giving her a proper funeral because of her uncle and mother.

Natalia's mother, Raquel, is so sweet and is beside herself that her daughter is gone. She doesn't know the real reason behind her death, and she never will. It would destroy her if she knew what Natalia was doing. The club has always protected them and made sure they both had whatever they needed, especially since Dr. Alvarez was one of the first members.

Natalia's father was a deadbeat and left Raquel when Natalia was a baby. Alvarez brought them to the States and cared for them until he came home and built a club here. Twenty years later, we have a thriving club, and Alvarez had his hands in a lot of other things besides the club, but I don't know what they are, and I don't want to know.

I flip through the channels on the TV, hoping something will catch my attention and distract me, and the channel lands on an American cooking channel. I miss some of these shows, and I zone out as I learn about the diners of America.

Voices echo down the hallway, filtering into the common room, alerting me that Church is over. I was a little untruthful when I told Ronan about the food. We need to go to Natalia's wake. It's a lot different from American culture.

I see Ronan walking out with Diablo, and they are talking about something and smiling. He looks up and sees me and winks.

"Hey, beautiful," he says as he sits on the couch.

"How did it go?"

"Pretty good." He's tight-lipped, and I know he won't tell me anything they discussed. "So, where's all this food you were talking about?"

"Well, um, I didn't say the food was here…"

"Rosalina, where exactly is the food?"

"At Natalia's wake."

"Is that like a visitation?"

"Yes, but they do it a little differently. Since Natalia's body got here, they took her to the mortician, and her body should be ready soon. Once she is in her casket, they will take her to her mother's house to be present for the vigil. All of her family will surround her and pray for 24-48 hours consecutively. Her casket will be open, and the room she's going to be in is full of pictures and memories of her."

"I see. So, do I have to pay my respects?"

"You should go to her mother and Dr. Alvarez. There are going to be many people there, and the food will be in a separate room. They also have games set up. It's an interesting way to celebrate the life of someone who has died."

"So, it's like a family reunion?"

"Yes." I snicker. "It's probably going to be loud too because it's the entire family, including children."

"Do I need to change into different clothing?"

"I'm going to change into something a little darker. Wakes and funerals are sacred, so traditional black clothing is expected."

"I have a black dress shirt that I'll put over my t-shirt."

"That will work."

We walk upstairs to my room. As soon as the door's closed, Ronan picks me up and kisses me roughly. I kiss him back, pulling and tugging on his clothes, wanting him inside of me to help me forget everything that is going on around us.

"Beautiful, I'm barely hanging on to what little control I have left," he breathes out between kisses on my neck.

"Lose control then."

He closes his eyes as he rests his forehead on mine. "I don't want to fuck you… I want to make love to you, but we don't have enough time."

"Tonight?"

He nods. "Yes, all night. I can't have enough of you…"

"Good." I smirk.

After a moment, we calm down, and Ronan places my feet on the ground.

"I'm going to touch up my makeup, then change my clothes. It shouldn't take me too long."

"Let me grab my bag out of the bathroom first so I can get changed while you're doing all of that."

Once he's out of the bathroom, I touch up my makeup, go to my closet, and pull out a black jersey dress. It is dressy but comfortable, so I put on a pair of black sandals.

I look at Ronan, who's on his phone. "I'm ready."

"Let's go. I'm starving."

"You're only going for the food, aren't you?"

"Correct, because Natalia can burn in hell for all I care." He shrugs.

"I'm sure you're not the only one who is going to be there that thinks the same as you."

"Oh, I know I'm not. But it is what it is, and I'd rather get it over and done with so I can come back here and get my dessert." He winks, and we walk downstairs to drive to the wake.

EDUCE

I wake up and roll over onto my side. Ronan isn't in bed, and I push myself up. Exhaustion fills every cell of my body, and I fall back into bed. Grief does something to your body, and it's hard to recover from it. Today is Natalia's funeral. Since her family is Catholic, they moved her body to the Catholic church that several of the members grew up in.

My mind wanders, and I think of the other night when Ronan made love to me. It was like something had totally changed between us, as if we had become closer and more connected. Now that we've fucked, had sex, and made love, I would pick making love almost every time. Ronan was so gentle, and the slow build of my orgasm, along with all the sensual touching and kissing... makes me wish he was here now.

I roll over on my stomach and attempt to fall back asleep, but I can't quiet my mind to sleep, so I get up. A hot shower sounds good, and then I'll get ready for the funeral. I turn the lights on and go to my closet to choose what I'm wearing today. Once that is done, I turn on the shower and wait for it to warm up.

The water is perfect, and I get in, letting the water wash over me. So much has happened in the past week. Natalia died and my relationship is amazing, and I'm sure the next step will be him claiming me as his ol' lady. He's had to talk to Ramiro about us, but he said nothing about that to me. Whenever the time is right, I'll know.

I wash and condition my hair and finish showering. Once I'm dried off, I put my hair in a towel, brush my teeth, and do my makeup. I'm just drying my hair and putting it in a bun so it's out of my face.

As I'm slipping my dress over my head, the door opens to my bedroom, and I turn around. Ronan walks in with a smile on his face.

"Hey, I was wondering when you'd be back."

He walks over to me and kisses the top of my head.

"I was talking to your brother and Diablo about the tech that Sledge sent to them."

"Nice. Have you already showered?"

"Yes. All I need to do is change my shirt, and I'll be ready to go."

"Make sure whatever you're wearing is comfortable."

"Yeah, it is, why?"

"It's a Catholic Mass service, and it will be long. There will be prayers for Natalia's safe travels into the afterlife, and it's very emotional. Don't freak out if you hear people crying out or sobbing. That's how many people express their grief at Mexican funerals."

"Will there be food after this?"

"Yes, a lot of food."

"I can make it through, then." He smiles.

"Prayer is an essential part of the funeral, so there will be prayers before and after Mass. Natalia's family will continue to pray for the next nine days for her safe journey."

"That's a lot of praying for someone who doesn't deserve it." He shakes his head.

"Maybe, maybe not. She's the one who has to answer to God." I go to my jewelry box and grab the rosary my father gave to me. I use it on special occasions.

While I finish getting my shoes on, Ronan changes his shirt and puts his cut back on. He checks his appearance in the mirror and is ready to go.

Once we are downstairs, everyone is ready to go. The ol' ladies aren't here, as they are helping prepare the food at Raquel's home. They will arrive at the church when it's time. We go to my Jeep, and I hand Ronan the keys. He fires it up, and we follow behind the Black Clovers MC.

The massive church overflows with people as Dr. Alvarez and Raquel are known in the community, as this is where their family roots began. We find our seats and a little after eleven, the first prayer begins.

Two and half hours later, Natalia Alvarez has been laid to rest, and I hope her soul is able to rest. There's a procession of cars, trucks, and motorcycles to Raquel's house, and I know she won't be left alone to grieve the loss of her only daughter.

The club has an area where they all are sitting, and

we join them. Ronan's phone rings and he pulls it out of his pocket and looks at the screen.

"I need to take this. It's Sledge."

"Okay." I smile at him as he gets up and walks to a secluded area.

"So, what's going on with you and Warrior?" Ramiro asks.

"We're dating and seeing where that goes."

"What do you want from him?"

"What kind of question is that? Do you want me to say I want his dick? Or do you are you looking for something else?"

"Watch your mouth, Rosalina," Ramiro grits out.

"I'm twenty-four years old, Rami, and I'm no longer a little naïve girl."

"I can still take everything away from you."

"Why are you threatening me for falling for Ronan? He treats me well. His kids are amazing, and he's a good guy."

"He's not controlling?"

"No, not at all. He's a lot like you, except for the mother hen hovering shit you do."

"You would tell me if he hurt you, right?"

"Jesus, yes, Rami. I would tell you, but I can take care of myself."

"Sorry, Rosa… I've felt lost without you here."

"I know. It's been different without you up my ass, but it's a good thing, too. Maybe you can find your ol' lady and finally settle down."

"No, thank you. Women are too much trouble." He chuckles. "I'm going to miss you."

"I know, but we will do a better job of staying in touch."

"Yes. That reminds me, your new phone is at the clubhouse. I'll give it to you later."

"Thank you." I get up from my seat and hug Rami. It was a struggle to let me go and trust another man to keep me safe.

"Let's find Warrior and get something to eat. I'm sure he's starving." He chuckles.

I believe I just received my brother's permission to be with Ronan, and I will not question him. I smile because I know how lucky I am to have a great brother and boyfriend in my life.

CHAPTER
TWELVE

Warrior

I experienced various ceremonies and rituals during my time in the military, but I had experienced nothing like what has taken place over the past ninety-six hours. The way the Hispanic culture views death is so different from home. Rosalina explained that there are holidays that honor the dead, too. It's a lot to take in, but I don't mind learning about Rosalina's culture. However, she said she didn't celebrate it much as her father passed very little of their culture down to her when he lived with them. She learned many of the traditions when she moved to Mexico with Jaguar.

When we returned to the club last night after the funeral, they had another party. They partied me out, and Rosalina and I went to bed. I'm sure most of the club was just going to bed when I got up this morning.

One thing I've found I like is the way they make their coffee. Super strong.

I let Rosalina sleep as she wants to go shopping with Maria later. Before coming downstairs, I lay in bed looking at her beautiful tan skin and wild, curly brown hair. Rosalina's gorgeous, and she's mine. I haven't compared her to Kelsey because I realized Kelsey was for a different chapter in my life. Rosalina is for the rest of the chapters in my life. I know we haven't been seeing each other long, but it feels right.

We are planning on leaving tomorrow if I can get Pappy out of the whorehouse. He's an ol' dog. I go into the kitchen, get a cup of coffee, walk outside, and sit in a chair on the patio.

"Good morning, Warrior," Jaguar states from behind me.

"Good morning, VP."

"See that you found coffee?"

"Yes, need it to wake up."

"That shit will put hair on your chest." He laughs.

"Tastes like Alvarez made it."

"We learned from the best."

"Yes, we did." I take a sip of my coffee. Before I can stop myself, I blurt out, "I'm claiming Rosalina as my ol' lady."

"Does she know?"

"No, but I believe she knows it's coming."

"Are you just claiming her?"

"I'll ask her. I'm fine with her being my ol' lady, but if she wants to get married, we will get married."

"And if you do anything to hurt her—"

"You'll kill me. I don't plan on doing anything to hurt her."

"Good." His face is void of emotion.

Great. I've pissed him off.

"I know you're protective of her, but I'm not some punk ass bitch. I've been with the club for ten years and worked my ass off to get my rank. Before that, I spent ten years in the Army, working my way up to get an honorable discharge. I saw how the assholes overseas treat their women, and I refuse to be one of those fuckers. And I'm too old for bullshit," I state, and he can take it however he wants to.

"At least you have balls, and I know she won't walk over you." He smirks. Asshole.

"And I won't control her. That's not who I am."

"You have my approval." He stands and offers me his hand. I stand.

"Thank you," I say as I take his hand and shake it.

"Everything in order to head back to Texas tomorrow?" he asks, sitting back down.

"Yes, I need to get back and make sure we have contained the Natalia situation to just the Ivory Wolves. However, we know they were in talks with the Cartel when they were here a few months ago."

"I tried reaching out to my father, but he isn't

responding to my messages. He normally has all the information in the cartels."

"If you get any information, please let us know."

"Definitely." He takes a sip of his coffee. "I'll let the ol' ladies know you are leaving in the morning. They will fix a feast for tonight."

"I think I've gained five pounds since I've been here."

"They love to cook. I'm sure we will talk later." He gets up and goes back inside the clubhouse.

I think I'm going to sit here and take a nap before it gets too hot.

By 6 p.m., the food is ready, and everyone is having a good time. I thought there was a lot of food at Raquel's, but there has to be double the food here for tonight. The ladies need to come to Texas and show us a thing or two about parties and amazing food. I would stay in Mexico just for the food because there is nothing like it at home.

I sit back with Rosalina on my lap and take in everything.

"How was your shopping trip with Maria?"

"Fabulous. I stocked up on products I can only get

here, and when I run out, she said she would send me more."

"Let me guess, makeup?"

She laughs. "No, well, maybe. Don't judge me, okay?"

"I'm not. I'm just trying to figure out where we're going to put everything."

"I'll make it work. I might need to get a storage unit…"

"Are you taking more stuff with you?"

"Yes, I'm getting the rest of my clothes, necessary paperwork, and some pictures."

"I have to let Pappy know."

"I already did. He said that it shouldn't be a problem."

"We probably should head upstairs and pack then."

"Yes, unfortunately."

Rosalina gets up from my lap and makes her rounds to people she wants to talk to and say bye to. I have a feeling we will make a trip down here a few times a year, and if it's always like this, I won't mind one bit.

I see her walking back toward me, and I stand to meet her.

"I'm ready to go pack now."

"Okay, let's go."

We walk inside the clubhouse and upstairs to her room. If I help her, she'll be done a lot quicker, and we can get to other things.

"I'll help you speed up the process."

"Okay, I have a lot of clothes and things to take with me, so your help would be appreciated."

She opens the door and turns on the light. There are a few boxes in here already.

"What's in those boxes?"

"The products I bought today."

I closed my eyes because I was wrong. This is going to take most of the night, and I will not be able to hear her moan my name before going to sleep.

"Do you have boxes for the stuff you want to take with us tomorrow?"

"Yes, they are in the next room."

"I'll get the boxes, and you go through your clothes. When you have the clothes you want to take, then we will box them up."

"Okay." She smiles and walks over to me. "Thank you. I know you don't want to be doing this, but it means a lot to me." She kisses my cheek and goes to her closet.

All the frustration I was feeling moments ago is gone. I get the boxes from the other room and come back with several for her to fill. She's making quick decisions, and it's going faster than I thought it would.

Two hours later, she had everything she wanted in twelve boxes. I'll have the prospects carry them to the van in the morning.

"Thank you, Ronan." She hugs me from behind.

I turn around and wrap her in my arms. "You're welcome. Are you sure that's everything?"

"Yes, I can buy it in Texas if I don't have it. I'm over packing."

"Good, because we're going to bed."

I pull her over to the bed and help her undress as she helps me undress, and I passionately kiss her and lay her on the bed. She pulls me into her, kissing me and rubbing her mound along my cock.

"Someone's a little needy tonight."

"Yes, you and those damn tight jeans. I can see the entire outline of your cock, and I think about all the delicious things it does to me."

"I love it when you talk dirty because it's so surprising coming from your mouth."

"I want to ride you until you come and can't take anymore, then you get hard again and come again."

Who the fuck is this chick, and where is my Rosalina?

"Um, yes, please!"

She smirks as she pushes me on my back and leans over on the nightstand for the condoms I stashed in there.

"Um, we're out of condoms."

"No, there's no way." I sit up and look. They're gone. What the fuck?

"I can go ask someone…"

"No."

"I'm on the pill," she softly states.

"Are you willing to take that chance?" I am still anticipating her following words.

"Yes," she says without hesitation.

"That's your hormones talking."

"No, it's not. Because I know if I get pregnant, you will take care of me and the baby. I'm not worried."

"Are you sure?"

"Yes." She leans over and kisses me.

"Rosalina Rodrígues, I officially claim you as my ol' lady. You're mine forever."

"Forever," she says as she pushes me back, aligns her core with my shaft, and slides down, bottoming out.

She raises her hips up and down, and her walls constrict on my cock with each movement as her orgasm builds. Her body is getting tighter, and she's almost over the edge, and I grab her hips, digging my fingertips into her flesh, and slam her down on my cock. I fuck her from below, thrusting into her as fast as I can, and she's crying out as she comes on my cock, and I don't let up. She wanted to fuck me until I came. Well, I'm fucking her until she comes again, then I'm going to make love to my ol' lady.

CHAPTER
THIRTEEN

Rosalina

I don't want to leave this bed. Every inch of my body hurts, not in a bad way, but in a thoroughly fucked way. Ronan doesn't enjoy giving control over too long, and my riding him turned into him fucking me, and then he made love to me as his ol' lady. He asked me if I wanted to get married, and I instantly said yes. There's no need to half-ass it.

That will be something we plan later on, and I want the kids involved, too. I hope that's okay with him. But I feel like all of this is too good to be true. How many people find someone they instantly fall in love with who's amazing in bed and treats you like a queen? Well, I guess the club is a good place to find guys like that. Maria said she's been in love with Diablo since they were in basic with each other and are still in love.

"Beautiful, what has you all wound up?" Ronan asks as he pulls me into him tighter.

"I'm just wondering if I'm going to wake up and all this is a dream." My mind races with all the what-ifs.

"What? Us?" His voice is gruff.

"Yes…"

He clears his throat. "This isn't a dream, although it might feel like one. I'm glad it's nothing like the dreams I have sometimes…"

"Dreams?"

"Nightmares."

"Do you want to talk about them?" I caress my hand down his chest.

He shakes his head. "Not really, because they are horrific, and I don't want you to be scared by what's in my head."

Oh, shit. What could it possibly be?

"I'm here if you ever want to talk."

"I know, thank you."

"You're welcome." I kiss his chest, then get out of bed.

I shower and get ready for the day. It's going to be a long one with the nine-hour drive. I'm surprised Ronan didn't join me in the shower. I notice he's on the phone when I step into the bedroom. That's why he didn't join me.

I try not to distract him and get dressed, and I put everything I'm taking with me in a box so I don't forget it.

"Fuck. I wanted to shower with you, beautiful," Ronan states as he places his phone on the nightstand.

"It's okay. There will be other showers, I'm sure."

"True." He gets out of bed, his erection straining against the material of his boxers. "I'm going to shower…"

"I'm all ready. While you shower, I'm going to see Ramiro. I'll wait until you come down to eat." I walk over to him, place my hands on his chest, and stand on my toe to kiss him.

"I'll be down shortly."

I nod and leave the room, quietly going downstairs and to the kitchen. Maria's already up and in there when I walk in.

"Good morning, Maria."

"Hey, good morning. Coffee?"

"Yes, please. Have you seen Ramiro this morning?"

"He and Juan are in his office talking about something. They should be finished soon. Neither of them has had coffee."

"How are they even functioning?"

"I'm not sure I wouldn't want to have a conversation with either of them…" She laughs as the door opens.

Juan and my brother walk through the door.

"What's so funny?" Juan asks as he gets two cups from the cabinet and places them on the table.

"We were talking about how grumpy you two are without coffee."

"I'm not grumpy." Juan glares.

"Keep lying to yourself." Maria shakes her head and then pours coffee into the cups. Juan takes one, and Ramiro takes the other.

"Are you all ready to go?" Jaguar asks, then takes a sip of coffee.

"Yes. I need help to carry my boxes downstairs," I state.

"I'll have some prospects do that now," he says. "Be right back."

However, he hesitates for a second.

"Are you sure you want to leave?" Ramiro quietly asks.

"Yes, I'm sure. I've made friends there, and I have more family now." I smile, knowing I'm making the right choice.

"You will always have a place here if you decide to return."

"If I come back, it will be with Ronan…" *You're mine*, comes to mind, and excitement floods my body.

"I'm just saying…"

"I know, but everything will be great."

The door to the kitchen opens, and Ronan walks through.

"Good morning, everyone." He smiles.

"Coffee?" Maria asks.

"Yes, please. Thank you," he replies.

"Breakfast is about ready. I know you need to get

going. Pappy has already been in here and back outside."

"Good. I was afraid that I was going to have to pull him away from the clubwhores." He shakes his head.

"Jaguar is getting prospects to get the boxes out of my room."

"I saw him talking to some when I came in here. After we eat, we should be ready to go."

"After all the boxes are in the van, I'll double-check my room."

He nods, then takes a drink of his coffee. He closes his eyes in pleasure. Yeah, the coffee is that good.

Maria places two plates of food on the table and we sit down to eat. I'm going to miss Maria and her cooking. I'm going to take this all in because I don't know when I'll have a meal made by Maria the next time.

Everyone comes out and hugs me goodbye. This is turning out to be harder than I thought it would be. Ramiro is the last person to hug me.

"I'm going to ask one more time. Are you sure?"

"Yes, I'm sure." I smile and lean up to his ear. "He claimed me as his ol' lady last night. That's forever."

"Yes, it is. But it doesn't mean I can't end it by ending his life," he whispers back.

"Keep your killing hand calm. I'm happy, Rami. Take care, te quiero." I hug him, and he hugs me back, not wanting to let go.

"Te quiero, please be safe. Call if you need anything."

"I will." I pull away and get into the van. Ronan shuts the door as a tear slides down my nose. I'm going to miss my family so much.

We pull away from the clubhouse and down the long drive that will take us to the main road. My heart is heavy, but I know that time will heal what I'm feeling. I remember when I left Arizona, and I wanted to go back to get my mom and bring her here almost daily. That feeling faded, and now I have to get used to being here without my mom and my brother. I'll get through it.

The drive back to Texas is much different in the daytime than at night. Even though the sun is shining, the motion of the van is lulling me to sleep. I grab the pillow and put it on the seat. I lay down, put the blanket over me, and allow myself to fall asleep.

CHAPTER
FOURTEEN

Warrior

I felt like someone was watching or following us when we left Tampico. I kept my eyes on the mirrors and checked everything out when we stopped for gas and food. My senses are usually spot on, but I see nothing that validates my feelings. I hate being tense and on edge. It's exhausting. When the walls of the club are in sight, my body relaxes. I've never been so glad to be home.

"Welcome back!" Wardog hollers as he opens the gate.

Pappy drives us through and around to the clubhouse. The van stops in front of the building, and my kids come running down the steps to meet me as I get out of the can.

"Dad!" Mason says as he runs and jumps on me, hugging me. "I've missed you so much."

"I've missed you too. Hey, Madison." She walks over and hugs me.

"Rosalina!" Madison runs over to Rosalina as she gets out of the van. "I missed you."

"Awe, I missed you too. Everything going okay?" Rosalina asks.

"Yes, but I want to talk to you later. It's girl stuff." Madison's face reddens.

"Okay, we can catch up once we get settled in, okay?" Rosalina rubs her back

"Yes, thank you." She smiles.

I grab our bags and head into the clubhouse, and everyone welcomes us back.

Sledge meets me at the bottom of the stairs.

"Go upstairs, and I'll be up in a second." The kids and Rosalina head up to our room.

"Welcome back, brother. We'll have Church to discuss what happened in Mexico at oh-eight-hundred-hours."

"Sounds good. I'm going to spend time with the kids and go to bed. It's been a long past couple of days. I'm exhausted."

"Fucking nonstop will do that to you." He smirks.

I chuckle and shake my head. "Yeah, that, too."

"See you in the morning."

"Yes, sir." I take the stairs two at a time and open the door to the room. The three of them are laughing.

"What did I miss?" I ask as I place our bags on the floor.

Mason turns around with his shirt over his head. There's a T-Rex head printed on his shirt. "I'm a T-Rex, rawr!" He stands up and comes after me like a dinosaur. The shirt makes it where his arms are shortened like a T-Rex, and I laugh.

"That is awesome, buddy. Where did you get that shirt?"

"Rosalina got it for me from Mexico."

"Look, Dad, Rosalina got me this bracelet." She holds her arm up for me to look at it.

"That's really pretty." I smile at Rosalina. She didn't have to get the kid anything.

"I know! She has great taste." Madison beams.

"Have you had dinner?" I ask Madison and Mason.

"Yes, Aunt June made us homemade pizza. It was so good."

"Brush your teeth and get ready for bed."

"Do we have to?" Mason groans.

"Yes, it's getting late," I state firmly. "We will be in to tuck you in shortly."

"Okay," they say in unison, then leave the room.

"Thanks, beautiful. You didn't have to get them anything."

"I know, but I thought they would like something small from Mexico." She smiles.

I pull her into my arms. "You're perfect, you know that?"

"I don't know about that..." She kisses me, and I passionately kiss her back.

"Let's go tuck them in and get something to eat."

"I like your way of thinking."

I grab her hand, and we first go to Mason's room and tuck him in. He doesn't want to take off the shirt Rosalina got him, so he's sleeping on it. Madison was all ready to say good night when we tucked her in.

We head to the kitchen, and I look in the fridge. June saved us some pizza. We heat it and go to the common area to sit at a table. I go to the bar and grab a couple of beers before sitting down.

By the time we clean up after ourselves, we are dead on our feet. The stairs to the room seem like a hundred, and the hallway feels never-ending. I open the door, and Rosalina walks in. She heads to the bathroom; I know now to do her routine.

She returns, strips out her clothes, and falls into bed next to me. I get up, use the restroom, and brush my teeth before stripping out of my clothes.

"Good night, beautiful. I love you," I whisper, and she doesn't hear me because she's already asleep. I pull her warm body into mine and drift asleep.

I get up, but I can't see. Everything around me is dark, and I feel like I am around the bed, and Rosalina isn't beside me. I look around and realize I'm not in my room. I do not know where I am. I walk around, then I run. I run until I see a bright light. The bright light. I recognize where I am, and I know what I'm going to see.

"Why are you torturing me?" I yell out.

I don't get an answer.

I stop running and walk toward the light. The white light is getting brighter and brighter, and I arrive. The exact figure sits in the light, and of course, I have to try to save her.

"You couldn't save me; no one could," Kelsey says as she holds a rusted razor blade to her arm, then slices upward.

I try to stop the bleeding, but there's so much blood. I cry out for help.

"Ronan, please, move on…" she whispers. "Save someone else."

The white light goes out, and I fall. I feel like I'm suspended in the air. Everything is quiet and peaceful. I feel safe here. A shot rings out—

"Ahh!" I yell as I sit up. I look around and realize I'm at home with Rosalina beside me.

"Are you okay, Ronan?" Rosalina asks.

"Yes, just had a nightmare."

I can feel her moving in the bed, and she turns on the lamp on the nightstand.

"We should talk about this nightmare…"

"I … I can't."

"Yes, you can. Please let me help you."

"I don't know where to start."

"At the beginning." She holds me tightly, and I know I'll be okay.

"Well, I met Kelsey in high school…"

And I tell her everything, knowing she probably will never look at me the same. She'll probably see that I couldn't keep my wife safe, and she'll regret being with me…

I wake up with Rosalina holding me. I've never been so vulnerable to a woman; she didn't take advantage of it. She told me she was proud of how I tried to help Kelsey and take care of her. She said she fell for me even more because I took what Kelsey was going through seriously. It made me feel better. Rosalina didn't see me as less of a person because I couldn't save Kelsey.

I get out of bed, stretch, and look at my watch. It's 6 a.m. Church isn't for a few hours, so I'm going to shower and head downstairs to grab something to eat before we meet.

We all file into Church, and it promptly starts at 8 a.m.

"This meeting has been called to order. Our brother Warrior has returned from Mexico and has information from his time there."

"Good morning, brothers. Pappy and I delivered Natalia's body to her family, and they gave her a proper wake and funeral as her mother didn't know the truth behind her death, and Dr. Alvarez wanted it to stay that way. The Ivory Wolves made a contract with the Cartel, and they know there is a bounty on Lana. Until we handle them, they will be a threat."

"Anything else?" Sledge smirks.

"I have a personal matter that involves the club. I have claimed Rosalina Rodrígues as my ol' lady. Jaguar gave his permission. She officially has moved here."

The room explodes with clapping and hollers.

"About fucking time, brother. We are happy for both of you."

"Thank you, Prez."

"So, lockdown is still in effect. We need to find those bastards and take them out. Slasher and the Steel Chains MC will stay until we can flush out the shit and dispose of them for good."

"Yes, Prez," the room responds.

"Warrior, get together with Slasher's guys and see if we can plan a trip to Mexico to stop these fuckers in their tracks."

"Yes, Prez."

Tyson's phone begins to ring, and he gets it out of his pocket. "It's the gate," he says and answers it. "What's up, Raider?"

"There's an old man out here claiming to be Rosalina's father."

"Warrior? Do you know anything about this?"

"No. Ramiro told me he was in hiding in Mexico." I shrug.

"Hold him there, and we'll be out," Tyson hangs up the phone.

"Anything else need to be discussed?"

The room is silent.

"Dismissed. Robo, check the cameras to make sure this isn't a setup. Warrior and Tyson, go out and see who he is. VPeep, have Scarlett get Rosalina and bring her downstairs to verify if he is her father."

"Yes, Prez," we reply.

We get in Tyson's truck and drive to the gate. There's an older car sitting on the other side of the gate and an older man standing next to Raider talking. When he turns around, I know he's telling the truth. He looks exactly like Jaguar, only older.

"Hey, how can we help you?" I ask as I walk into the gatehouse.

"I want to see my daughter, Rosalina."

"Are you Eliso?"

"Yes, how did you know?"

"Rosalina is my ol' lady. I thought you were in Mexico hiding?"

"I was, but I heard Rosie was here, and I wanted to see her..."

"I'll let you in, but I don't know if you can stay or even if Rosalina would want to see you."

"I'm willing to take that chance," the old man states.

"Let him pass,"

I command. The gate opens, and he gets back in his car.

I don't know how Rosalina will react, but I hope I don't regret this.

CHAPTER **FIFTEEN**

Rosalina

I hear a lot of talking, but I can't make out if it's real or if someone is listening to their TV loudly. I roll over because I'm not about to get into someone else's business. Someone knocks on the door as I'm drifting back to sleep. I wake up as they knock again. Before I answer the door, I grab one of Ronan's shirts and put it on.

"Hey, Scarlett. What's up?"

"There's a man downstairs who claims to be your father."

"My father's in Mexico."

"That's what he said. Warrior wanted me to come and get you to verify this guy's story."

"Okay. Let me throw some clothes on. Come in." She shuts the door behind her.

I pick out a clean pair of shorts and a tank top, go to the bathroom, and freshen up before wearing clean clothes.

My hair is messy, so I pull it back in a messy bun to keep it out of my face.

"Let's go find out who this guy is."

We walk downstairs, and the guys are surrounding a table. I spot Ronan and walk over to him, club members stepping out of my way.

"This man stated that he's your father," Ronan states, and the man looks at me.

"Papi?" I look at the man who looks like an older version of Ramiro.

"Hija!" he states as he stands. I walk over to him and hug him.

"What are you doing here, Father?"

"Ah, it's a long story, but I heard you were here and want to see you. It's been too long."

"So, is this man your father?" Sledge curtly asks.

"Yes, this is Eliso Rodrígues, my father."

"Okay, go into the conference room and talk, okay?"

I nod, and Warrior shows us to the room and shuts the door behind him, leaving me in here with my father.

"What are you doing here?"

"I overheard some talk that you were here, and I wanted to see you."

"It's not very smart for you to come here and put the club at risk, Papi."

"I won't stay very long. It's been too long since I've seen you."

"Yes, I know, but that's because you're always on the run."

"I know, but my life is ending soon, and I wanted to make my amends to you."

"Are you dying?"

"Aren't we all?"

"You can't answer a question with a question."

He sighs. "I'm not dying in the sense of cancer or anything like that. As soon as the Cartel finds me, I'm dead. There are a couple of clubs that want me dead, too. I'm a dead man walking." He chuckles.

"I don't think that's hilarious. If any of those organizations find out you are here, they will attack a club that has nothing to do with."

"I know, and I tried to be very careful when I came here. They won't know that I came here."

"If you say so. Are you hungry?"

"Yes, and thirsty."

"Okay. I'll get us something and bring it back in here." I get up, leave the room, and walk through the common room. Warrior's sitting on the couch, playing on his phone. He looks up.

"Everything okay?"

"Yes. Getting food and drink."

We walk into the kitchen, and he makes sure no one's around.

"I'm letting you know Sledge clarified he doesn't

want your father here because it will bring trouble to the club." He hugs me.

"I figured. Papi said he was leaving tonight. He is on the run from the Cartel because he ripped them off and two MCs."

"Fuck. He needs to get out of here."

"Yes, I need to let Ramiro know, too."

"I'll call him, and you spend time with your father. Be firm with him. He needs to leave soon."

"I will."

He kisses my forehead, then helps me make sandwiches.

Ronan helps me carry everything to the conference room, and my father's sitting there half asleep.

"Papi, we brought food." I smile, and he opens his eyes.

"I'll bring more cold drinks in a bit, Rosalina," Ronan states, then closes the door.

I watch as my father picks at the food that we made, and I wonder when the last time was he had an actual meal.

When I was younger, he was in the good graces of the Cartel and the MCs. He often ran drugs or guns for them, using his business as a coverup to get product wherever it needed to go. Something must have changed. My father looks so old, but he's only in his 50s.

As he swallows the last bite of his sandwich, he opens a water bottle and drinks it all.

"Thank you, Rosie. That was good."

"So, what changed? Why are you being hunted now?"

"I'm tired. I tried to get out of the game, and they wouldn't let me. They said the only way that I could stop working for them was if I was dead."

I gasp.

"So, I took a shipment of it and sold it to someone else, bought cheaper products, and gave them to the MCs. The MCs thought the Cartel had ripped them off, and it started an issue between them. So, they sent more products, and I did the same thing again. I was making millions off of the deal, too. The second time, they figured out what I had done, but I was already long gone when they tried the other bricks of dope. But I was proactive before I made the second run. I cleaned out my shop and my house. I bought the car I'm in under a fake name and in cash. Everything I own is in that car."

"Oh, Papi. Why did you even get started with the Cartel?"

"The money was substantial, and I could do what I wanted, when I wanted, as long as I made sure the drugs went to the right people. But then the border patrol tightened up, and people couldn't be bought anymore."

"Why not turn yourself in and go to prison?"

"The Cartel has guys on the inside. I'd rather die on my terms, not theirs."

"I understand," I say as my stomach rolls. This probably will be the last time I see my father.

"Are you still hungry?"

"I could eat a little more." He smiles.

"I'll have Warrior make us some more sandwiches and extras to take with you."

"Thank you. Sounds good."

I stand up to leave the room.

"Rosie?"

"Yes, Papi?"

"I'm proud of the woman you grew up to be. I'm so thankful your mother took good care of you and Ramiro." A tear escapes his eye, and he quickly wipes it away.

I lean over and hug him.

"Thank you, Papi. That means a lot." I smile at him, then leave the room.

I lean against the hallway wall and slide down it. Why is death always the only option in this world? I let the tears fall, knowing I'd never have a relationship with my father.

CHAPTER
SIXTEEN

Warrior

Eliso being here concerns me greatly, especially after she told me the Cartel is after him. I let Sledge and Tyson know what we are dealing with, and Sledge wants him out of here by dark since Robo confirmed what she told me. The conference room is bugged, and he's listening to them talk.

I haven't seen her since, so I hope she's there telling him goodbye. Ramiro needs to be made aware of what's happening, so I go to the office, share with Tyson, and shut the door. And call him on a secure line.

"Rodrígues," he answers.

"It's Warrior."

"Something up?"

"Yeah, your father is here."

"Fuck."

"Sounds like he's in all kinds of trouble. He told Rosalina that he fucked over the Cartel and two MCs, both have hits out on him."

"Fucking dammit. Why couldn't he just keep his head down?"

"I'm not sure, but I want to help him get back into Mexico to somewhere safe."

"That's not possible. If the Cartel is after him, he cannot return here, which is probably why he's there. Did he say why he came there?"

"He overheard Rosalina was here." I put my elbow on the desk and put my head in my hand.

"Get him the fuck out of there!" he yells through the phone. "He probably heard that from the Cartel. They are looking for her to pay for what he's done to them."

"Fuck me. Okay, I'll get him out of here now. Thanks." I close my eyes. I allowed him to come right in and probably lead the Cartel to the club.

"Yeah. Let me know how it goes."

"Will do." I hang up the phone and go to Sledge's office.

I knock on the door. It's partially open.

"Come in, it's open," he states.

I push the door open more and stick my head in the room. I don't have time to sit down and chat.

"I'm getting Eliso out of here now. Jaguar stated they were probably looking for Rosalina to pay for what Eliso stole for them."

"Get it handled."

"Yes, Prez," I say, pushing the door almost closed.

I head to the conference room and knock on the door. A few moments later, Rosalina opens the door.

"Times up, beautiful. I need to get your father on his way."

"Okay, he was getting ready to leave."

"Thank you, young man, for allowing me to spend time with my little girl. Please take care of her," he states as he holds his hand out for me to shake.

I grasp his hand. "I will, sir."

Rosalina hugs her father, and they walk outside with his bag of food and drink in his hand. He gets in his car and drives toward the gate as the horizon darkens. The gate slowly opens, and Eliso goes through it. He turns his signal on, and a fire ball erupts from the car, shaking everything as it knocks us to the ground.

"No!" Rosalina cries out, and I grab ahold of her as another explosion rocks through the club. The gatehouse is destroyed, but the prospects are about to get out and put the floodgate up. They would need something powerful, like a tank to knock it down.

"Get the women and children to the bunker!" Sledge yells as we run into the clubhouse.

June takes control and gets everyone downstairs to the bunkers set up under the club.

"Someone get over to the other building and get the Steel Chains over here."

"On it," Wardog states and disappears down the stairs.

Sledge gets on his phone.

"Robo, what do you see?" Sledge asks as he gets everyone together to plan the attack.

"Four trucks with ten plus guys in the back and one rocket launcher. Looks like the Cartel."

"I fucking knew they would follow Eliso here," Sledge angrily states. "This shit ends tonight. Robo, are they surrounding the club, or are they centralized in one area?"

"Looking now… I'm not seeing movement on the other cameras, so they are at the front gate, attempting to get through."

"Will it withstand a rocket attack?" I ask.

"It was tested for gunfire, and it held up. Someone has to be pretty ballsy to come at us with a rocket launcher," Robo states from his dungeon. His office becomes a safe room when we are under attack so we can have intel.

The Steel Chains MC comes up the stairs and meets us in the common room.

"What's going on?" Slasher asks as he checks his pistol and puts it back in his holster.

"The Cartel paid us a visit," Sledge grits out.

"Good, now we don't have to waste time looking for them." He smirks. "What are we looking at?"

"Forty-plus guys and a rocket launcher. Not sure of what else they have."

"Plan?" Slasher asks.

"Since these guys are fucking morons and didn't do

their research on the club property, we sneak out the back and come up from behind them, taking most of them out before they know what hits them. Then we will send a message back to the head of the Cartel…"

Slasher rubs his hands together. "Nothing like a little torture to send a message loud and clear."

Sledge smiles. "Fuck yes. Snaps?"

"Yes. Prez?"

"Take out the fucker that is trying to blow up my gate."

"Yes, sir." He grabs his gun case and heads downstairs.

"We will split up half and half. My guys will show your guys where to go," Sledge states. Tyson, take one group and go around to the west side. Warrior takes the other group and goes to the east side. Call when you're in place."

"Yes, Prez," we answer, and head down the stairs, dividing each other up before we make it to split in the tunnel.

"Stay safe, brothers." I fist-bump Tyson, and we head off in the opposite direction. We reach the stairs leading to the door outside a few minutes later. I climb them and press the video camera to look out before opening the door. There is no movement or anything out there. I quietly open the door and usher everyone out, then I make sure the door is locked behind me and push it shut.

We make our way around to the east side of the

front of the building, and we are on the east side of the parking lot of the BCMC bar. Eliso's car will be in between us once everyone is in position. My eyes land on the trucks, and I count forty-eight bodies. The gatehouse remains continue to burn and I'm glad the prospects could react quickly. I think I'm recommending a full patch for them.

I make sure we are in place and call out the sound of a Whippoorwill, and a few moments later, the responding call comes out from the west side of the parking lot. Everyone is in position, and we will aim south when we open fire.

When Snaps takes out the rocket launcher prick, we will open fire on everyone else. We wait.

The third Whippoorwill call comes out, and that's our cue that Snaps is ready and preparing to fire. A single shot rings out, and yelling ensues. I fire, and everyone else does the same. The guys in the truck are scrambling, trying to figure out where we are shooting from. Snaps continues to pick them off one by one until there's no more movement. I hold my hand up to cease fire.

We hold our position until we are given an all-clear.

"Clear," Snaps shouts from the roof of the bar.

We get up and cautiously walk up to the trucks, guns drawn. No one survived.

"I guess we will send these dead bodies as a message," Tyson states and laughs.

"I don't think they were expecting us to have the

numbers. Thanks to our brothers in the Steel Chains MC for fighting with us," I state to them.

"Welcome, brother," echoes through the crowd.

The floodgate opens, and Snaps and Sledge walk out with Slasher.

"Looks like they handled business," Slasher states.

"This should get the message across," Sledge states. "Get this shit cleaned up and put that car fire out."

"Yes, Prez."

It will be a long night because the prospects can't do all this, but I will check on Rosalina first.

"I'm going to check on the women and children."

Sledge nods, and I head to the clubhouse to tell them it's clear. I need to hug my ol' lady and my children.

CHAPTER
SEVENTEEN

Rosalina

Everything was going well, and it was too good to be true. My father's dead, and I don't know how I feel. He abandoned us when I was in middle school. My father didn't want to be a father. He wanted to come and go as he pleased because he was too selfish. I want to break down, but I can't. I need to stay strong for Madison and Mason, who haven't let go of me since we've been down here.

There's a beeping, and the door opens. June and Scarlett pull out their guns and point them at the door.

"Clear," Warrior yells out as the door finishes opening.

They lower their guns, and Warrior walks in. Madison and Mason let go of me and run to their father. Grief kicks me hard in the gut. I will need to call

Ramiro to let him know what happened. Then, one of us will have to call Mom, a call that I don't want to make.

"Hey, beautiful, how are you holding up?" he asks before hugging me.

"I'm really numb right now. I don't know what I should do or how I should be feeling."

"I'll call Ramiro and get him up here so you can work through this with my support."

"You think that's a good idea with the Cartel after me?"

"I think they will hold off on bothering you right now. They killed your father, and we killed forty-some of their men," he states, and I nearly fall.

"Whoa, beautiful. I got you. Let's get you upstairs." He holds me as we walk through the tunnel.

"Okay. Is it okay if the kids sleep with me?"

"Yes, because I don't know when I'll go to bed, and I'd feel better knowing that you all are together."

"Thank you."

"Come on, kids. Let's get upstairs. You can have a slumber party in our room."

"Awesome!" Mason shouts as we walk up the stairs.

"I need to call my mom, but I still want to talk to Ramiro."

"That's fine. Use the landline in my room."

"Okay."

"I'll get the kids in their night clothes while you make the calls so you can have some privacy."

"Thank you."

I open the door to our room and close it behind me. I'll call Ramiro first. I dial his number, and he answers quickly.

"Rodrígues."

"Romi, Papi's dead."

"Fuck!" I hear things crashing on the other end of the line.

"The Cartel attempted to come in. They blew up his car and were trying to get inside the club."

"I knew something stupid like that would happen. I'll leave here in a bit and be there by sunrise."

"Okay. I'll call Mom."

"She'll probably want to bury him there."

"I, um, don't know if there will be anything to bury..." I say as tears stream down my face.

"The brothers will get it handled. This isn't the first time we've had something like this happen. I'll be there when you wake up. Te quiero, hermana."

"Te quiero, Romi. See you soon."

The next call is to my mother. I dial her number and don't know if she will answer from this line.

"Hello?"

"Mom?"

"Rosie, what's wrong? You're crying!"

"Papi... Papi is dead," I cry out.

"My God, no! Are you sure?"

"Yes. I saw it with my own eyes. He was here in Texas, and the Cartel got him..."

I hear her crying through the phone. She never stopped loving my father.

"Can he be brought home?"

"I think so. Rami is on his way here to get everything in order."

"Okay, have him call me once he knows what is going on, and we will plan everything."

"Sounds good, Mom. I love you."

"I love you, too. Please keep me up to date."

"I will."

"Thank you." She ends the call, and I sit here, numb, lost, and confused about why people around me have to die.

Ramiro arrives the following morning, and all the evidence of what happened the night before is gone. Except there isn't a gatehouse anymore. Warrior stated they would build it back by the end of the week.

Once Rami talks to Sledge, VPeep, and Warrior, the clean-up company could get my dad's bones out of the car. They put them in a casket and are waiting for us to let them know where to send it.

Mom and Rami work on the funeral plans, and we are having a private funeral for my father. We are going to drive to Arizona, bury my father, and come back. It's easier not to be noticed if you drive.

When we arrive in Arizona, it feels like I haven't been home for a lifetime. My mother is upset because I didn't call her about my relationship status change. I guess I'll let her know whenever we get engaged when that happens.

Rami forgoes the traditional Catholic Mass funeral and just has a short and simple "we will see you when we see you" funeral. We had said goodbye to him long ago, and there was no need to rehash all of those old feelings.

We stay with Mom for a few days to make sure she's doing okay, then come back to Texas. I thought Rami would be gone the following day, but he stays. We've talked a lot and worked through emotions that happen when working through grief. I'm going to miss him so much when he goes back.

When I walk in from spending time with the kids outside, I notice that he is getting comfortable with Phoebe. She would be suitable for my brother, but I don't want him to string her along. She's been hurt too much to be dicked over.

"Hey, you two," I say, sitting on a chair beside the couch. "What are you watching?"

"Nothing, we are just talking."

"Oh, I see. I won't interrupt you then. Rami?"

"Yea?"

"When are you going home?"

"In a few days. Why?"

"Making plans with Ronan and the kids. I didn't want to miss spending time with you."

He smiles, and I get up. I want Phoebe to know that he wasn't here for very long. It probably was a dick move, but I don't want to see her hurt. I go upstairs, grab the kids, and watch a movie with them.

I'm so glad they are in my life. I love spending time with them, and they help ease the pain of losing my friend and my father in less than a month. They remind me that life goes on, even when it's rough. These two are thriving after losing their mother at a young age. They are still working through the emotions of that, and together, we will heal.

CHAPTER
EIGHTEEN

Warrior

Holy fuck. If I don't travel for the next year, I'd be happy. Well, traveling to funerals because those things are exhausting. I'm cranky because I haven't been inside of my ol' lady for over a week. A week too long. Jaguar went back to Mexico, and hopefully, I can get back to taking care of my ol' lady.

I want to be selfish and have Rosalina all to myself. I need to bury my cock deep inside of her, fucking her until she's screaming my name. But I'm going to wine and dine her first, touch her, tease her, then take her to bed where we don't have to worry about being interrupted.

I head downstairs to see if I can find Scarlett. I hope she can watch the kids overnight and make sure they behave. Voices are coming from inside the kitchen. I open the door, and Scarlett and Savannah are discussing what they are getting Sledge and Ava for the baby.

"Hey, ladies," I say, walking into the kitchen.

"Hey, Warrior, how's it going?" Scarlet asks as she's making a cup of coffee.

"Good. I have a favor to ask of you." I pull out a chair at the table and sit down.

"Yes, I'll do it. Tell the kids to come downstairs, and we hang out in the game room." She smiles.

"How did you know?" Women and their freaky déjà vu shit.

"It's been a few weeks since everything went down. You need some alone time with Lina, and I'm free tonight. John is going on a run." She shrugs.

"Thank you so much. And there's something else I want to talk to you both about." I look from Scarlett to Savannah.

Savannah's brow raises. "Yes?"

"The kids and I have been working on the perfect marriage proposal for Rosalina. Even though she's already my ol' lady, the kids want to ask her to marry me. They want her to be their mom officially. I think it's awesome, and I like how they love her as a mother, but they're not trying to replace Kelsey with her. So, can you help me set up a party or something for next weekend?"

"Yes!" both say.

"Everyone loves Lina. I'm so glad that you, too, got

together," Savannah states and walks around the table, hugging me.

"Nothing too fancy because she isn't that type of person."

"We'll keep it simple. Maybe cheesy." Savannah smirks.

"Sounds good. Thank you, ladies." I get up from the table and head upstairs to wake up Rosalina.

I walk into the bedroom and turn on the nightstand lamp. Rosalina lays on her side, with the sheet draped over her front, back, and arms exposed.

"Hey, beautiful, wake up." I lean down and kiss her cheek.

She mumbles incoherently.

"Rosalina, come on, beautiful. I have a surprise. You need to get up and get dressed. We're going out of town." I kiss the top of her shoulder, and she stretches.

"What did you say?" She's half awake.

"I'm taking you somewhere so we can spend time alone together."

"What about the kids?" she mumbles.

"Already handled."

"Okay, I'll get up and get ready." She yawns.

"I'm going to tell the kids about us leaving and that Scarlett will be spending time with them," I say as I run my fingers down her arm, causing goosebumps.

She nods, and I kiss her, then leave the room to wake Madison and Mason. They have been sleeping in lately, and I believe it's because Rosalina has them outside doing things and spending time with them instead of being on their fucking phones. I hate those damn things sometimes.

After talking to both kinds, they're excited to spend time with Scarlett because she's the aunt with a potty mouth. I'm so glad that's why they like her more, not.

I go back to the room, and Rosalina's in the shower. I won't bother her because I'll have her all to myself soon. I pull my phone out of my pocket and look for exclusive hotels in San Antonio with everything in one place. The less driving I have to do, the more time I have to be with Rosalina.

The duffle bag I packed for Arizona is still on the chair, so I grab it and dump the contents, putting fresh clothes inside it. By the time I'm ready, Rosalina comes out of the bathroom with a towel around her body and hair.

"What made you decide we needed to do something like this at the last minute? This isn't like you," she questions as she looks through her clothes.

"I need to spend time with my ol' lady and not be interrupted by children or club members."

"That sounds wonderful. I thought you're getting too tired to care for me, ol' man." She walks over to me and kisses me on the cheek.

"Oh, beautiful, I'll show you ol' man tonight."

"Can I have a sample?" she smirks.

"Is that a new term for a quickie?" I chuckle.

"Yes, it makes it sound so delicious." She drops her towels, showing her tanned, curvy body to me.

I unzip my jeans and push them down far enough to release my cock and balls from my boxers.

"Come here, beautiful." She does. "You know the drill. Wrap your arms around my neck." Her hands go in my hair, and I grab her ass and roughly push her against the wall, causing pictures to fall. "Sorry."

"I'm okay." She smiles.

I pick her up, and she wraps her legs around my waist. While pushing her against the wall, I take my hand and tease her slit with my cock, coating the tip with her wetness. I align myself to her core and slam into her. She moans as I thrust into her, and I kiss her hard, drowning out the sound. I don't want the kids to hear me fucking their soon-to-be stepmother.

"This sample is almost over, baby. Rub your clit so you can come with me," I rasp out.

Rosalina moves her hand from my hair and moves it in between us as she rubs on her clit, and her walls tighten around my cock.

"That's right, baby. Feel me pounding into you. I'm going to fill you up with cum," I breathe out. Rosalina comes hard, and I feel her wetness coating me, triggering my release. "Oh, beautiful." My forehead rests on hers. "I can't wait to make you scream my name tonight." I wrap my arms around her ass and carry her to bed, laying her down.

I go to the bathroom to get a washcloth to clean

myself and her, too, and I walk out to the room and spread her legs, cleaning her up so she can get ready. Something so simple can be so sexy. I love caring for her.

"Mi amour, where are we going?" she asks as she gets up from the bed.

"It's a surprise. Dress comfortably."

We say our goodbyes to the kids, get everything in my car, and drive to San Antonio. I can't wait to have her underneath me.

A week after spending the weekend alone with Rosalina, we have a family day planned in Houston, and it's the big day. The kids, Scarlett, Savannah, and I have been planning this proposal and party for a week. I'm nervous because she could say no. She could want just to be my ol' lady because she would have an out, but I hope not.

"Kids, Rosalina, you ready to head to Houston?" I ask. They are huddled around Rosalina's computer screen.

"Yes, we're ready." Rosalina looks at me and smiles.

"What are you looking at?" I try to see over the kids' heads.

"Colleges. I think I might apply once I can see if I can afford it." She shrugs.

"Go if you want to. I'll make sure you have the money to go if you want to."

"I can't take your money—"

"Our money. If you want to go, then go."

"Okay, I'll figure out which would work best for us." She bites her lip.

"You. The one that works best for you. I'm here to support you in whatever you decide."

Rosalina smiles at me, then states, "Let's get going so we can enjoy our time together."

The drive to Houston seems to take forever, but time flies by once we reach our first stop. We ate lunch and explored some sights, then we played putt-putt. The kids beat us both, but we had a fun time losing. Our last stop is the Waterwall for the proposal. I haven't been here before, but Scarlett and Madison came up with the idea. I'm glad Madison is coming out of her shell.

We pull into the park, and we're speechless. The wall is u shaped and at least sixty feet tall with water cascading down. In front of the waterfall is a wall shaped like a house with three arches. A big, open grassy area allows you to walk or do whatever with the waterfall in the background. I park the car, and we get out, walking toward the Waterwall. The kids run ahead of us, running around in the grassy area, burning off some of the energy they have.

"This place is amazing," Rosalina states as she walks around, and I grab her hand.

I look for Madison, and she's looking at me. I nod, and she knows it's time for the proposal. They made signs and put them in her backpack to get out when it was time. They run to the façade and yell for us.

"Come closer. It's so awesome!" Madison yells. She turns around and walks to the other side of the façade with Mason, and I know they are getting their signs ready.

We walk on the concrete, and I see Mason peeking around the corner. I pat my pocket to make sure the ring is in there, and we are good to go.

Madison walks out, and Mason follows, holding their signs.

Rosalina sees them, and her hands go to her face, covering her mouth.

"Will you marry our dad?" Madison asks.

"Yes! Yes, I'll marry him!

She turns to me, and I get on one knee. "Rosalina, you've brought so much light into our lives, and we would be honored if you would be my wife and their mother."

"Yes, I will. I do. All of it!" she yells.

I slip the ring on her finger, and the rosy, red rubies and diamonds shine in the sun.

"Picture time!" Madison states as she takes picture after picture.

"I love you, Ronan," Rosalina as she gets down on the ground with me and kisses me.

"I love you, too. Let's get back so we can celebrate property." I wink because I mean a party, and I'm sure she's thinking of sex.

Everything is quiet when we pull into the club and enter the clubhouse.

"Congratulations!" Everyone yells as confetti shoots in the air and cat calls ring out.

"How did you know?" Rosalina asks.

"Girl, we've been planning this for a week." Savannah snickers. "And we made traditional Mexican food. Jaguar hooked us up with recipes."

"Hopefully, Maria's," she states.

"Yes, and she even Zoom called us to make sure we were doing it right. She was a hardass about doing everything the right." Scarlett laughs, and then she turns a little green. "Excuse me." She runs to the bathroom.

VPeep comes up and shakes my hand.

"Oh, I hope she's okay?" Rosalina asks.

"She is fine—just some tummy issues. Congratulations, I'm glad you found someone that makes you this happy," VPeep states.

"Thanks, brother."

"A toast!" Sledge calls out. "To continued growth of the Black Clovers family. May God bless us with good health, good sex, and, of course, good whiskey."

"Cheers!" the room erupts.

I see Scarlett walk back in from the bathroom with a cheesy smile on her face. She gets VPeep's attention, and she whispers in his ear. His eyes widen, then he looks at me. VPeep leans over to me.

"Hey, I don't want to ruin your engagement party… but I have an announcement."

"Okay." I smile because he is the VP, and it's not like I can say no.

"Can I have everyone's attention?" The room quiets down. "Since we are all here, I wanted to share some other news… Scarlett—"

"We're pregnant!" she yells.

The room goes nuts, and that's the end of calming anyone down. The party will probably continue all night long, but Rosalina and I will be going to bed and celebrating our engagement in our way.

I hope that one day, we'll get to announce that we are having a baby of our own.

EPILOGUE

Rosalina

It's been two weeks since Ramiro returned to Mexico, and I want to call to check in on him, to make sure he's doing okay, and to tell him I got engaged. Plus, I want to tell him I'm thinking about going to college to become a teacher. There is something about it that calls to me, and I want to give it a shot.

I pick up my phone and hit send when I see his name and face.

"Hola, hermana."

"Hi, how are you doing?"

"I'm good. I rested up after that trip. That was crazy."

"I know, right? I still can't believe Papi is gone."

"He was living on borrowed time. He did many people wrong, but he also did many people right."

"I guess that's one way of looking at it. So, guess what happened?"

"What?"

"Ronan and his kids asked me to marry him. It was super cute," I blurt out.

"Congratulations!"

"You knew already, didn't you?"

"Maybe."

"He asked for permission?"

"Twice."

"I guess he really loves me."

"I'd say so." I can hear his smile through the phone. "Have you checked your checking account lately?"

"No, I've been trying to save my little money."

"Check your account later on."

"Why?"

"Just do as I say, okay?" He chuckles.

"Fine. So, guess what?"

"What?"

"I'm seriously considering going to college to become a teacher."

"That's great! Do you know where you're applying?"

"No, just looking about programs right now."

"Well, good luck. What does Warrior think about it?"

"He's really supportive and believes I would be a great teacher."

"I agree."

"So, what about you and Phoebe?"

"Not this again. You know I'm not interested in settling down right now."

"You should because you have someone to keep you warm at night and to fuck your brains out."

"You didn't just say that!"

"I sure did. It's wonderful, and I thought you should know." I snicker.

"I don't need to know about your sex life, Rosa," he breathes into the phone.

"Of course you do. You said you wanted to keep tabs on me, so I'll tell you everything."

"Keep that information to yourself, okay?"

"Fine, I will. Get laid. You might feel better."

"Jesus. I'm going to let you go. Don't forget to check your bank."

"I won't."

"Te quiero, hermana."

"Te quiero," I reply, and he ends the call.

I open my computer and look at teaching programs again, because this is a great time to return to college. There are so many schools, and I get lost in all the programs and applications; I don't realize that three houses have passed. I better look at my checking account before Ramiro calls.

I log in, and I can't believe my eyes. I must be in the wrong account, or some deposited into the wrong account. I log out and log back in. Oh my God! There are 2.7 million dollars in my account.

I call Ramiro back.

"Where the hell did the money come from?"

He chuckles. "Dad, he left us eight million, and I'm going to deposit it slowly for you."

"I can't."

"I know. I guess he cared for us after all."

"What about Mom?"

"She got even more. It's in a safe deposit box."

"I'm speechless."

"Te quiero, Rosie. We'll talk soon."

"Te quiero, Romi."

I used to think that Mexico was my home forever, but I realized it was a temporary place to get me where I truly belonged, which is here, with Ronan and his children. Looking back on everything that got me where I am today, I've lost a lot. But I've gained a lot as well.

I'll begin online classes in a few weeks, and I'm excited to start this new journey with Ronan by my side.

"Beautiful, the one day I get to sleep in, and you're

awake and trying to figure out world peace," Ronan mumbles as he stretches underneath my body.

"Sorry. I was thinking about everything…"

He chuckles. "Rest, beautiful. You'll wish you had more lazy Saturdays when you start college."

"You're probably right, but I'm wide awake and hungry."

"Food sounds good. What kind of food do you want?"

"Let's make pancakes, bacon, and eggs. The kids will like that, and I'm sure everyone else will. It's easy to make a lot."

"Let's get going then."

I move off his chest, and he pulls me back down, kissing me passionately as I moan into his mouth.

"There, that's a proper good morning." He smirks.

"Good morning to you, mi amor."

I get out of bed, not caring to put any clothes on, and go to the bathroom to turn on the shower. The hot water will wake me up and make me feel good about my sore body. I pull my hair back before checking the water and enter the steamy shower.

The water beats down on my back, releasing the tightness I had across my shoulders. I turn around and get the front of my body wet, and I hear Ronan get in the shower behind me.

"Took you long enough."

"It's hard to get out of bed with a boner."

I snicker. "Sorry, I guess."

"No need to be sorry. I'll have you work it out later."

I turn around and face him, my arms going around his neck. "You're not going to fuck me in the shower?"

"Not this morning. I'll make it up to you later."

"Are you sick?" I take my hand and place the back of it on his forehead.

"No." He chuckles. "I thought of somewhere I want to take you, and it would be the perfect place to make love… Delayed gratification, beautiful."

"That sounds exciting." I smile as I wonder where he might take me.

"It will be. Hand me your poof so I can wash your body."

"No hanky panky, Mister." I attempt to scowl at him, but fail miserably.

"Yes, ma'am."

Ronan takes his time washing my body, and my desire for him burns at my very core. I wash him, showing him the same detail he showed me, and as I finish, he pushes me against the shower wall and kisses me.

"Thanks, beautiful." He rinses off and gets out of the shower.

I give myself a final rinse and get out, drying off in the bathroom before I finish getting ready. I walk out into the room with my towel wrapped around my body. My clothes are still in boxes, so I dig through a box to find shorts and another to find a tank top. My underwear and bras are in the dresser already.

Ronan is lying in bed, already dressed in shorts and a cutoff shirt. Mmm. The shirt is slit deep down the side, and it allows me to see his muscular chest and tattoo that I love tracing with my tongue.

"Beautiful, if you keep looking at me like that, I'm going to have to fuck you. It would be over too quickly, and you'd be cranky. You're hungry for food, so let's get downstairs."

"You're bossy."

"And you like it," he says, getting out of bed and walking over to me. He kisses the top of my head and opens the door for us to go downstairs.

No one's in the common room. Most of the members are probably sleeping off the alcohol from the party last night. We walk into the kitchen, and it's spotless. I'm sure it won't be for long. I get out everything I need for the pancakes, and Ronan gets the bacon and eggs.

"You make pancakes, and I'll make the bacon and eggs?" he asks as he pulls out the griddle, a couple of cookie sheets, and a large pan.

"That works."

I whip up the pancake batter and let it rest for a few moments. While waiting, I make coffee and pour Ronan and me a cup before the pot can fully brew. The coffee's warmth wakes me even more, and I make several dozen pancakes.

Within an hour, the almost empty kitchen fills with people as they smell the bacon cooking. The kids come down shortly after most of the club. I made them special pancakes and set them to the side. I put the bacon in the pancake because I wanted theirs to be special.

A few others volunteered to clean up since we did all the cooking, which was fine with me. I hate doing dishes.

We sit in the common room. Most of the officers are in here except Tyson. He and Lana have been at their house since the lockdown was lifted. Dr. Swartz doesn't look like she feels well.

"Ava, are you feeling okay?" Savannah asks as she plops down beside me on the couch.

"Yes, just exhausted. Ready for this little one to make their appearance." She looks like she could use some sleep.

"How much longer?" I ask.

"Any day now." She rubs her belly.

"I'm excited because I'm going to make sure they are spoiled." Savannah claps her hands.

"Just remember that, Savannah. I'll be calling you when they are screaming their head off because you spoiled them." Sledge shrugs.

"That's fine. They will love their Auntie Vanna." She sticks her tongue out at Sledge.

Dr. Swartz gets up from the couch, steps, and stops as something hits the floor. Did she just pee?

"My water broke," she mutters.

"The baby's coming?" Sledge shouts.

"Yes, take me to the clinic."

He picks her up, and we follow them to the clinic.

"Lina, I'll need your help," Scarlett states as she pulls me into the emergency room that's set up in the clinic. "Savannah, get the tech set up in here in case we need to video Dr. Alvarez," she orders.

"What do you want me to do?"

"There are blankets in the warmer out in the hallway. Get several of those and towels out of the cabinet."

I nod and run into Snaps out in the hallway.

"Sorry." I get everything and place it on the cart that Scarlet is reading next to the bed Dr. Swartz is on.

Snaps helps Savannah set up the tech, but they seem to have different opinions on how to get it done.

"That's now how I was shown to connect that, Snaps. Stop and let me do what I have to do," Savannah says as she pushes him out of her way.

"Why do you have to do everything the hard way?" he questions her.

They keep going back and forth.

"Savannah, Snaps, get out of the room and go finally fuck each other. Maybe that will settle the both of you down," Dr. Swartz snaps, and the room quiets.

Oh shit.

"You heard her, get out," Sledge orders.

They leave the room, neither looking at Dr. Swartz nor Sledge.

"Ava, I need to see how far you're dilatated," Scarlett says, and I kind of zone out.

Blood and bodily fluids are not my thing, and I stand back as Scarlett and Lana, who showed up a little bit ago, deliver Dr. Swartz's baby.

I step outside of the room as she begins to push.

"Everything okay?" Ronan asks as he gets up from the chair, comes over, and wraps his arms around me.

"Yes, the baby should be here soo—"

The door flies open. "It's a boy!" Sledge shouts. "Adrian James Lewis and he's healthy." Hoots and hollers fill the waiting area, and then he goes back through the door.

"That was fast," he states, then kisses me on the head.

"Yes." I smile, hoping that if I get pregnant, it goes that easily.

"So, what's your thoughts about having our baby?"

"I stopped taking the pill the day you told me I was your ol lady." I look up at him, our eyes meeting.

"You weren't going to say anything?" he questions.

"I didn't know how to. It's only been a few weeks…"

"Hmm. After we make sure everyone is good here, we are going home to practice making babies."

"Babies?" My eyes widen.

"Oh, yes. I'm thinking we can have at least two more." His smile can get me to do whatever he wants me to do.

"I think one will be enough." I giggle.

"We'll see." He winks.

I walk back into the room, making sure Dr. Swartz is stable, and the baby is doing well. Once I know I'm no longer needed, I leave the room and let Ronan know that the baby and mom are stable.

We leave the clinic hand in hand. The touch of Ronan's hand in mine educed a feeling of love and desire I've never felt before, and I hope the feeling never goes away.

BOOKS BY A. GORMAN

Black Clover MC Texas

Emanation

Evoke

Educe

Their Sins Series

Rules of Her Sins

Blackmailed

Double Cross

Coming soon

Unwanted Series

Unwanted Orders

Unwanted Fate

Ryan Crime Family

Black Clover

Black Night

Black Clover MC Ireland Origins

Casúir

Standalone

Love, With All My Heart

ABOUT THE AUTHOR

A. Gorman is an author who writes whatever the characters in her head dictate. Becoming an author was never in her plans, yet she finds immense joy in transforming the stories she conceives in her mind into tangible works for others to devour.

Social Media
Website: http://authoragorman.com

- facebook.com/AGormanAuthor
- x.com/AuthorAGorman
- goodreads.com/annagcoy
- tiktok.com/@agormanauthor

www.ingramcontent.com/pod-product-compliance
Ingram Content Group UK Ltd.
Pitfield, Milton Keynes, MK11 3LW, UK
UKHW031007240225
455493UK00012B/965